DARK
SPELL

DARK SPELL

GILL ARBUTHNOTT

 Kelpies

Kelpies is an imprint of Floris Books
First published in 2013 by Floris Books
© 2013 Gill Arbuthnott

This publisher acknowledges subsidy from
Creative Scotland towards the publication
of this volume.

 This book is also available
as an eBook

British Library CIP data available
ISBN 978-086315-956-5
Printed in Poland

*For James and Calla, who let me steal
their house (again)*

For Nessie, who got all the best lines

And for Raffaella and the cast and crew of
Winterbringers, *who inspired me.*

PROLOGUE

I am living in a nightmare. There is nothing but fear and darkness and noise. I feel the weight of the earth above me, pressing down, waiting to devour me.

The candles flicker. Please, God, don't let them go out and drown me in darkness.

I would lay down the pickaxe and crawl out of this hole into the light, but the commander would kill me with as little thought as he would give to the killing of a rat. There is nothing I can do but dig.

Perhaps hell will be like this.

1. VALENTINE'S DAY

"Imagine what it must have been like," said Mr Davidson. "Kept in a dungeon for weeks, then dragged out and tied to a stake..." he paused for dramatic effect, "...and burned alive! That's what happened to George Wishart, just a few hundred metres away, in 1546. But why?"

He looked at the rows of faces in front of him, waiting in vain for some sort of response.

A hand went up.

"Yes, Evie?"

"Has anyone sent you a valentine card, sir?"

Mr Davidson flushed slightly. "This is a history lesson, Evie."

Evie Carroll gave a theatrical sigh. "I was only asking."

"You all live in St Andrews. Surely you know *something* about the history of the town?" Mr Davidson ploughed on determinedly.

The faces looking at him were perfectly blank. He swallowed nervously. There was a snigger from the back of the classroom.

Callie Hall, sitting near the back herself, thought, *Why are they doing this? He's only a student teacher, he hasn't done anything to them.*

"Come on, some of you must have ideas." Mr Davidson licked his lips and swallowed again.

It was like watching people torture a kitten. Callie felt her fingers start to tingle as her annoyance grew. She had had enough. She put down her pen which, strangely, kept rotating gently on the desk in front of her, and put up her hand to answer.

"It was religion," she said. "Protestants and Catholics."

Mr Davidson gave her a look of such naked gratitude that she was embarrassed. She looked down, caught sight of her pen, still turning by itself, and grabbed it.

"That's it exactly, Callie. Cardinal Beaton, who was Catholic, had Wishart, who was Protestant, burned as a heretic. But Wishart's friends took revenge..." He turned to write something on the board and half the class swivelled round to glare at Callie.

"You moron," hissed Jessica Langston. "Why did you spoil it?"

"She fancies him or something," said Evie under her breath. "*She* probably sent him a valentine card. She's such a loser."

Callie did her best to ignore them, and to ignore the prickling in her fingers, and stared at the board until the bell sounded for the end of the lesson and the start of lunchtime.

She contemplated eating outside somewhere, but although it was bright, it was pretty cold. It was only February after all.

The school cafeteria was full of girls giggling over valentine cards and eyeing up boys. Some of the boys were sniggering over cards too. Callie wondered fleetingly if Josh, her friend in Edinburgh, had sent anyone a card or got one himself. She couldn't imagine him behaving like these prats, but maybe he was different in Edinburgh to how he was here.

She found a quiet table and fished her lunch and a book out of her bag. She was absorbed in both when she heard a voice in front of her.

"Got a date with Davidson yet then?"

It was Evie, lunch tray in hand, backed by the rest of the posse that seemed to travel everywhere in her wake. They all wore matching sneers.

Evie put her tray down.

"Next time there's a plan, don't screw it up, you freak." She picked up her cup of water and threw it in Callie's face. "Oops. Sorry."

A ripple of laughter ran round the room as Evie picked up her tray.

Callie watched through her dripping hair as Evie walked away, anger building inside, fingers, hands, every inch of her tingling now.

At that moment Evie seemed to slip, though there was nothing on the floor: no pool of water, no smear of ketchup, no uneven floorboard. She screamed as she went down hard on her back, the contents of her tray flying up, then falling, to land with improbable accuracy all over her.

The posse squealed in horror and hurried to help her.

Callie dried her face and her long, brown braid of hair with her scarf, and went back to her lunch, ignoring the pool of water on the table in front of her.

"What did you do to her, freak?" Callie hadn't seen Jessica stomping over. "How did you make her fall?"

Callie felt heat rising in her face as she looked at Jessica and beyond her to Evie, who was screeching and carrying on as the posse helped her to her feet. She seemed to be holding her wrist.

"How could I have made her fall? I was over here, you know that. She just slipped." Even as she said it, she could feel the treacherous prickling in her fingers again. *Not now, oh please, not now...*

The posse ushered the sobbing Evie past her, some of them shooting venomous glances at Callie.

"This is your fault, loser!" one of them shouted.

"I don't know what you did, freak, but we'll get you back for this. Just wait," Jessica spat at her as she turned to go.

Callie watched them leave, fighting the prickling, trying to calm herself. On the table, the spilled water bubbled and steamed unnoticed.

As she sat on the bus to Pitmillie after school, she replayed the scene over and over in her head.

The way Evie had fallen... the way the food had landed all over her...

The aftermath, when people had realised she was howling because more than her pride was hurt and she was taken off to hospital with a suspected broken wrist.

It's not my fault. It's not my fault.

How could it have been her fault? She'd been nowhere near Evie. Evie had slipped, no one had pushed her, least of all Callie.

It can't be my fault.

IT'S MY FAULT.

They were right. She was a freak. And there was no one she could tell.

"Anyone in?" Callie called as she opened the front door. Chutney Mary, her tortoiseshell cat, came trotting to meet her, tail high, purring like an engine. She bent to stroke the cat's head absentmindedly as it butted against her legs in greeting.

"No one but us, puss?"

Callie made herself a cheese sandwich and settled down to work, or at least tried to. She found she couldn't concentrate, still seeing Evie's fall in her mind. After half an hour she gave up and set off for her grandparents' house.

Rose and George Ferguson lived in one of the oldest buildings in the village. It had been the smithy for at least two hundred years before they turned it into a house. Callie opened the front door – it was unlocked as usual – and peeled off her coat as she went in.

"Rose? George? Where are you?" She turned on the hall light.

There was a soft whine, and an enormous dog rose from his bed in the hall and came over to have his head scratched: Luath, the family's Scottish deerhound.

"Are they in the garden?" Callie asked the dog. He tilted his head to one side as though he was deciding how to answer her, then gave a short bark as he heard the back door open.

"Hello," Callie called.

"Hello dear," said Rose, appearing with an armful of old newspapers. "Cold today, isn't it? Go and light the fire and I'll put the kettle on. George is just finishing something in the greenhouse."

"Okay."

As Callie walked across the hall the lights flickered briefly. Rose glanced at them and pursed her lips, watching her granddaughter as she walked away. Luath pushed his massive head against her thigh.

"You can feel it too, dog, can't you? You're just too polite to say anything."

She got rid of the papers and several layers of clothing and bustled about with cakes and biscuits and the all-important teapot. Her mind, though, was elsewhere. *Callie. This can't go on much longer. The power is getting stronger.*

"I said, do you want a hand?"

Rose jumped as she registered the voice.

"Er... no, George. It's all fine. Go and see if Callie got the fire to light."

An hour later, fortified by tea and lemon drizzle cake, Callie put her coat back on. She felt much calmer; being with Rose and George usually made her feel better. They understood far more about her than her parents did.

"School all right just now?" Rose asked casually, putting the remains of the cake back in the tin.

Callie made a face. "No worse than usual. But people are just... incredibly *annoying* sometimes. I hate the way you're not meant to show you're interested in class. It's just a few of the girls really, but everyone copies what they do. Well, not everyone, but a lot of people."

"Ah," said Rose. "It's easy for me to say, I know, but you go your own way. Don't follow them like a sheep."

"As if!"

Rose smiled. "I thought not. Away you go. Your mother will wonder where you are."

"She'll know I'm here."

"I suppose she will. Remind her about the cake sale in the church hall on Saturday. She said she'd make something."

Callie snorted. "That'll be the day."

'Now, now. Off you go."

When Callie got home a few minutes later, the lights were on and the TV was blaring out the news. She could hear the shower going.

"Hello?"

"I'm in the kitchen." Her mother's voice competed with the newsreader's, and won.

Chutney Mary appeared at Callie's side like a familiar, and they went into the kitchen to find Julia, Callie's mother, bending to check something in the oven.

"What's for tea?"

"Pasta bake."

"Homemade?" asked Callie hopefully.

Julia shook her head ruefully. "There wasn't time. Sorry. We're only just in. Dad's in the shower. Have you been over at your gran and grandad's?"

Callie nodded. Although she always called her grandparents Rose and George, and had done so since she first learned to talk, her mother never acknowledged it. Weird.

"Rose said to remind you about some cake sale."

"Oh no. I forgot all about it."

"Just tell her you're too busy."

"No," said Julia, with a frown of resolve. "It's for the village hall roof. I'll find time to make something tomorrow. Clinic finishes early; I should be able to do it."

Callie's parents were both doctors. Her mother worked in the hospital in Dundee and her father was a GP. Cake making was not high on the list of priorities in their house.

"How was school?" Julia asked.

"Fine," said Callie.

"Anything interesting happen?"

"No."

"Did you talk to anyone today?"

"Of course. I don't go through whole days without speaking."

"You know what I mean, Callie. Don't turn everything into a confrontation. It's just a question."

Callie rolled her eyes. "*You* know I've got nothing to talk to them about." She headed out of the door. "I'm going on the computer to do my homework. Tell me when tea's ready."

She logged on to Facebook and found a message from her friend Josh.

Hi Callie
Your art trip sounded fun – not!!
Loved the skateboarding pig on YouTube – ta for the link. You should try to train Chutney Mary to do that ha ha.
Off on school ski trip tomorrow, and I've never skied (if that's how you spell it) before. Bet I break both legs.
Back end of next week.
Mum's talking about heading up to Pitmillie again this summer. Hope you're going to be around?
Josh

It was pathetic, Callie thought as she replied. Surrounded by people her own age five days a week, and her best friend was a boy who lived in Edinburgh who she'd met for two weeks last summer.

They'd been thrown together by circumstances and found they got on really well, although on the surface they had absolutely nothing in common. Since then, they'd kept in touch on Facebook and met up once, when Callie went down to Edinburgh to do her Christmas shopping. Maybe she could go down again at Easter.

Hi Josh
Try not to break too many bits!
Yeah I'm around most of the summer.

Might come down to Edinburgh at Easter to see you on your crutches ha ha ha.

Callie

Rose Ferguson stared at the water in the washing-up bowl. The face that stared back at her wasn't her own, but that of her friend and fellow witch, Bessie Dunlop.

"What's the matter, Rose?" said the wavering image.

"It's Callie. There's no doubt any more. She was here this afternoon. I could feel it crackling out of her like static and she made the lights go dim."

"But she doesn't know yet?" As Bessie tilted her head, the water sloshed to one side of the bowl.

Rose shook her head. "But she'd used her power today without knowing she'd done it, Bessie. You couldn't miss the traces. Even George could tell something was up."

Bessie Dunlop was not a woman to mince her words. "Then we have to – *you* have to – tell her as soon as possible so that we can get her trained. We can't have her ricocheting all over St Andrews leaking power everywhere."

"It's not so much telling Callie that worries me," Rose admitted. "It's telling Julia." She made a harrumphing noise. "If I didn't remember giving birth to her I'd find it hard to believe she's my daughter. I think she's still ashamed of me, you know. She certainly used to be when she was Callie's age and she'd just found out what I was. I thought she'd get over it when she inherited, but when she didn't, it just got worse and worse. I don't want her making Callie feel like a freak."

"Keep calm, Rose. You're making the water steam at this end. She'll come round," said Bessie, trying to sound reassuring.

"You don't know how stubborn my daughter can be."

"Well, she certainly can't be any more stubborn than you."

Rose didn't rise to the bait.

"Will you tell Barbara and Isobel what's going on? We need to find a date when you can all come here, as soon as possible."

"Don't you worry, Rose. We'll all do this together."

"Thank you, Bessie."

"Who are you going to tell first?"

"Callie. If I told Julia she might up sticks and move just to avoid the truth."

"Surely not?"

"Well, maybe not, but I wouldn't put it past her to ship Callie off to some boarding school."

"Well, we can't have that. You know," Bessie mused, "it's a shame that Hogwash place doesn't exist."

"Hogwarts, Bessie, Hogwarts. And can you imagine what it would *really* have to be like? All those untrained children... they'd reduce the place to rubble in half an hour. It would have to be built like a nuclear bunker, not a castle."

They had a good laugh at that, causing little whirlpools to form in their watery images, before Rose said, "Well, I'd better go. Let me know when the others are free."

Bessie's image faded, and Rose was left staring at her own reflection once more.

Callie pushed open The Smithy's garden gate and Luath rose from the frosty grass to greet her with a welcoming bark.

"Hello, dog. What are you doing out here in the cold?"

She waited for the dog to follow her in through the front door, but he lay back down.

"Suit yourself, you daft animal."

Callie dumped her coat on the bottom step. "Rose?" she called.

"In the kitchen."

"Oh – hello," Callie said in surprise when she went in, for not only was Rose sitting at the kitchen table, so were her old friends Bessie, Isobel and Barbara. Callie had known them all her life, but Rose didn't usually ask her to come over when they were there.

"Sit down, dear," said Rose.

She looks nervous, thought Callie. *What's going on here?*

"Have a piece of chocolate cake." Bessie pushed a plate towards her. "Isobel baked it, so it's delicious. Much better than Rose's. I'm sure Isobel would share the recipe if you asked her nicely, Rose."

Rose bridled visibly before she realised that Bessie was trying to provoke her, to distract her from her nerves. She poured Callie a cup of tea and watched as she cut herself a slice of chocolate cake.

Callie felt four pairs of eyes on her as she cut the cake. Why did this feel like an ambush?

She took a bite and made suitably appreciative noises. It *was* good, but not better than Rose's.

"How are things at school?" asked Bessie brightly. "Everything going well?"

"Same as usual," said Callie slowly.

What was going on? They *all* looked nervous now. Her fingers began to tingle.

Rose licked her lips.

"We wondered if you'd noticed anything... unusual... happening? You know... anything strange... any odd feelings?"

Callie stared at Rose and the others, trying to pretend she couldn't feel the prickling sensation surging up her arms now.

"No," she said, in a voice that didn't even convince her.

"It's all right. It's nothing to be frightened of," said Isobel.

"We've all had it," Barbara added.

Callie felt as though she couldn't breathe. She was going to pass out.

"What do you mean?" she gasped.

"You're like us, dear," said Bessie.

Callie looked helplessly at Rose through the cloud of sparks dancing in front of her eyes. The feeling of pressure in her head, her arms, her hands was becoming unbearable. She couldn't stop it... she felt as if she was going to explode.

"You're a witch, Callie," said Rose.

"No!" yelled Callie, slamming her hands flat on the table as she surged to her feet. There was a loud *crack!* and the table burst into flames.

2. WITCH

Luath howled, a long mournful note. The front door of The Smithy opened and emitted a faint cloud of smoke and a coughing Bessie. Luath howled again.

"Quiet now, dog. There's no harm done, just a lot of noise. You see why we sent you out here?"

The dog wagged his tail and sank back on his haunches, for all the world as though he understood. Bessie disappeared back inside, leaving the door ajar.

The scene in the kitchen as she came back in was one of determined normality, like a smile through gritted teeth. Barbara and Isobel were concentrating very hard on washing-up, and ostentatiously paying no notice to what was going on round the table, which bore no trace of its fiery ordeal.

Callie sat, white-faced and trembling, Rose's arm round her shoulders.

"What's wrong with me?" she sobbed. "I'm a freak. I'm a monster. What's happening to me?"

"You're no more a monster than any of us, my darling," Rose said firmly. "We've all been through this. You're a witch like we are, but you don't know how to use your power yet, and it can just... flare up like that. There's no harm done. Look, the table's not even scorched."

"I can't be a witch." Callie's voice rose. "There's no such thing. Why isn't the table burned?"

"If there was no such thing, the table wouldn't have burst into flames. It was your untrained power that set it alight. But we thought something like that might happen, so we'd prepared the room – put protective spells on it."

"And sent the dog out where he'd be safe," Bessie interjected. "So you didn't accidentally barbecue him. Singed dog is not a pleasant smell." She sounded as though she was speaking from experience. "Try not to panic, dear – everyone's the same when they find out. I can assure you you're not a freak – unless you think the four of us are freaks?"

"Dangerous ground, Bessie," called Isobel from the sink, as she and Barbara dropped the pretence that they weren't listening avidly to what was going on.

"Forget about *Meg and Mog* and *The Wizard of Oz,*" said Rose, "and it might be a bit easier to believe. Real witches aren't anything like that. They're just normal people, like us."

Callie looked dubious.

"But you're old. Witches are old. I'm young. I can't be a witch."

Rose saw Bessie gathering herself to take offence.

"We were actually the same age as you, once," she said hurriedly. "And we were witches then too."

"You need to forget everything you've ever read about witches," said Isobel.

"Or seen in films," added Barbara.

Bessie glanced round the kitchen. "In fact, I think it's about time that Barbara and Isobel and I went home."

A few minutes later, Rose and Callie sat alone at the kitchen table.

"This isn't some sort of crazy old-person joke?" Callie asked, hoping against hope.

"No, dear," replied Rose, carefully ignoring the insulting part of the question. "But you already know that, don't you? You've noticed things happening."

Callie nodded, looking miserable, then blurted out, "I think I broke someone's arm at school."

Rose waited quietly for the story to tumble out. When it reached its end, she said, "You didn't break the girl's arm. You didn't even *mean* to make her fall. This doesn't make you a bad person, Callie, but it does show you why it's important that we train you to use your power, otherwise things like that will just keep happening. I know this has been a shock. You need time to take it in properly, then we'll start your training."

"What about George? Does he know what I am?" She paused as a thought occurred to her. "Does he know that *you're* a witch?"

"Well, he knows most things that go on in this house, but it's easier for everyone if he doesn't have to admit to it. Of course he knows what I am, but we don't discuss it. I think he'll have a fair idea about you too, even though I sent him off to Fife Ness to keep him out of the way just now."

"And Mum and Dad – how am I going to keep things secret from them?"

"Ah." Rose looked uncomfortable. "I don't think

your father's likely to notice. His mind doesn't work that way. Julia's another thing."

"She's not...?"

"Goodness, no."

"Does she know about you?"

Rose nodded. "And disapproves of me thoroughly because of it. We'll have to tell her of course, but not just yet. Wait until you've got used to the idea."

"When I'm about your age, then?"

They both laughed, a bit shakily.

Callie logged on to Facebook and stared at the screen. Nothing new. She'd been hoping that there might be a message from Josh – he should be back from his ski trip by now – but obviously he was far too busy having a real life. Unless he'd broken both arms and couldn't type. Nothing from any of her other so-called friends either.

It was probably just as well there was nothing from Josh. She might have been tempted to tell him what was going on.

Yeah, that would work well...

Hi Josh, how are you? By the way, did I mention I'm a witch? That's right, I really am a freak.

It was a few days since Rose's kitchen table had burst into flames, and Callie was still battling with herself over whether to believe what Rose had told her.

On the one hand, it couldn't be true, because there were no such things as witches – not now, at least, although she'd discovered last summer that one of her

25

ancestors, a girl called Agnes Blair, had supposedly been a witch. But on the other hand, it explained so much.

She'd been trying to ignore the tingling, and the accompanying feeling that she was some sort of human kettle coming to the boil, for months now. It had all started when Josh was here last summer, and had been getting steadily worse ever since. It was a relief to get any explanation for it, however unlikely.

Callie turned back to her computer and opened iTunes, determined not to go downstairs: Rose had arrived ten minutes earlier to talk to Julia about her, and Callie certainly didn't want to be in the same room when Rose broke the news. She could feel her fingers prickling at the thought.

Cautiously, she held her hand out over her desk, pointed her fingers at a pen, and spoke.

"Move."

The pen remained resolutely immobile. Callie sighed. She must have tried this, or something like it, two dozen times since she'd found out what she was, and nothing had ever moved. Behind her, unseen, a postcard dislodged the drawing pin that held it and fell off her noticeboard.

She stiffened as she heard raised voices from downstairs. It sounded as though Rose had reached the point of the visit.

A few seconds later, her mother shouted up the stairs, "Callie?"

She crossed her fingers and pretended she hadn't heard.

"Caroline, come down here now!"

There was obviously no escape. Reluctantly, Callie dragged herself down to the kitchen.

Rose sat, thin-lipped, clutching a mug of tea as though it was an anchor in a storm, while Julia glared at her.

"Whatever your grandmother's told you, I want you to forget it. It's nonsense," Julia spat out as soon as Callie entered the room. She stared at Rose, daring her to say anything, but Rose held her peace.

"It's not nonsense," Callie said quietly. "I've known there was something wrong – something strange, anyway – for months. It made sense as soon as Rose told me."

"Callie, this is rubbish. You're not a witch."

"Are you going to tell her there's no such thing, Julia?" Rose asked. "Even you don't really believe that. So, since you acknowledged years ago that I'm a witch, why won't you believe that Callie's one? You know that it can skip generations."

"I won't have this happen to my daughter."

"You don't have a choice, and neither does Callie. She is what she is. I'm not asking you to be happy about it; just don't make things difficult for her."

An uneasy silence descended on the room. Rose got up to leave.

"Please, Julia. Think about what's best for Callie."

"Do you think I don't usually do that?" Julia retorted angrily.

"You know that's not what I meant." Rose sighed. "I think I'd better go now."

"Yes."

When Rose had gone, Julia and Callie stared at each other.

"It's all rubbish, Callie. Everything these old women have told you. Don't let them suck you into all this. You've got a normal life to live, just like everyone else."

"But I want to understand what this is, what's happening to me."

"*Nothing's* happening to you. You're just growing up. Of course there are times when everything seems strange. Ignore it, and you'll soon forget all about it and get back to normal."

"I want to find out about it. This is happening to me, Mum, whatever you want to believe."

"Do you want me to have to tell your father what's going on?"

Callie raised her eyebrows. "If that's a threat, it's not a very good one. You wouldn't do that. You'd have told him about Rose long ago if you were ever going to talk to him about witches. Mum, this is happening. Face it."

Callie and Rose sat at Bessie Dunlop's kitchen table in St Andrews, as they had done twice a week since the confrontation with Julia a month before. Bessie put a blue and white striped teapot and two stubs of candles in the centre of the table and sat down.

The two women stared at Callie.

"Well?" said Rose.

"Aren't you going to light the candles?" asked Callie.

"No dear, *you* are."

"Where are the match... Oh. Right. Of course." Callie

wriggled herself comfortable and leaned forward in her chair, concentrating on the candle wicks. Rose and Bessie sat very still so they wouldn't distract her.

Callie stared, frowning, at the candles. After a few seconds, wisps of smoke came from the wicks, then tiny, buttercup-yellow flames that grew and steadied.

"Good girl!" exclaimed Bessie.

"Now the net, Callie," Rose urged her. "Remember what to do?"

Callie nodded and, standing, reached for the tips of the candle flames and drew them up, longer and longer, strands of living flame that somehow didn't burn her. She twitched her fingers and twisted the flames together into a shining filament, then, tongue poking out as she concentrated, waggled her hands as though she was playing with an invisible cat's cradle.

The filament became a net the size of a mixing bowl, suspended between her hands.

"That's it..." Rose said encouragingly as Callie prepared to flick the net of light over the teapot.

For the first couple of weeks she hadn't been able to do any of this. When she tried to control the tingling, the lights would flicker or the radio would howl with interference, but nothing more. She remembered how astonished, how elated she'd been the first time she managed to focus her power on a candle and saw the wick bloom into a flame.

It was all going so well.

But in remembering, she'd let her concentration waver for a second and the flame forgot it couldn't burn her. She gave a yelp of pain and yanked her hand away from the net, which detonated with a *snap* and a whoosh of sizzling air.

There was a *crack* and the spout fell off the teapot.

They stared at it sadly.

"I'm sorry," said Callie indistinctly, sucking a burned knuckle.

Rose tried not to show her frustration with her granddaughter's failed attempt at this simple piece of magic.

"Ach, don't worry, Callie. I can soon mend that," Bessie reassured her.

"With magic?" Callie asked, brightening at the possibility that witchcraft might actually be some use.

"Dear me, no," said Bessie, rummaging in a drawer. She produced a small tube and held it up triumphantly. "With superglue."

"I'm never going to be able to do any of this properly," said Callie gloomily. "I'm not even sure I *want* to. What's the point of all this stuff with the net? I didn't ask to be a witch. I'd rather just be normal. Surely if I don't use whatever power I've got, it'll just... fade away or something?"

Rose sighed. "I keep telling you it doesn't work like that. Untrained power can be very dangerous. Even if you choose never to use it, you have to be able to control it."

"Mum says if I ignore it, it'll go away."

Bessie looked sideways at Rose, then concentrated very hard on glueing the teapot.

"I wouldn't pay too much heed to your mother as an authority on witchcraft," Rose said in a tight voice. The two of them were barely on speaking terms because of what was going on.

She shook her head as if to clear it. "Let's stop for today. We've been at it for over an hour anyway. You *are* getting better, Callie. You just need to let your power flow more freely. Don't worry, it's hard for everyone at first."

"I had to give up cooking for two months when I was learning," Bessie interjected. "Everything I made came out smelling of wet dog. I still have no idea why."

"I never knew that," said Rose, trying to hide a smile.

Bessie sniffed haughtily and put the repaired teapot down gently. "It's not something I like to dwell on. My brother teased me about it for months. Barking Bess, he used to call me. Before I turned him into a slug."

Callie looked at Bessie, wide-eyed.

"Och, I'm joking dear. It's no challenge fooling you; you need to try a bit harder not to believe everything I tell you!"

Callie gave an uneasy laugh. She was never quite sure about Bessie...

Rose stood up. "We'd better head off before we break anything else."

"Sorry about your teapot, Mrs Dunlop."

"Bessie," said Bessie. "We're all witches, and I keep telling you that witches are all on first name terms. And the teapot's fine anyway."

With a tiny thud, the spout fell off again.

3. THE TUNNELS

```
Just about 2 leave.
C u this afternoon?
```

Josh watched the envelope icon sail across the screen as he pressed *Send*. He was looking forward to seeing Callie again, of course, but to his surprise he was getting slightly nervous. What if they had nothing to say to each other face to face? Facebook wasn't the same as spending actual time with someone.

He looked at the pile of bags and boxes in the hall and took his headphones out.

"You don't mean *all* this, do you?" he shouted to his mother, Anna, who was filling yet another bag in the kitchen.

"Yes. It'll all fit in if we pack the boot carefully."

"I didn't realise we were going for three months." Josh poked around in a couple of the bags. Blankets. Why was she packing blankets? It was shaping up to be the warmest summer for years and she was taking *blankets*?

"Are we still going to Pitmillie, or did you change the booking to Iceland and forget to tell me?"

Anna emerged from the kitchen with a bag in one hand and a list in the other.

"Ha ha. I'm not taking anything for granted after last year. I've never been so cold in bed in my life as I was then."

"But..."

"Never mind *But*. Just shove it all in the boot. Carefully."

Sometimes there was no point arguing.

"So when do I get to meet this boy?" demanded Julia as she shoved a load of washing into the machine. "You're being very secretive about him."

Callie cringed at the tone of her mother's voice.

"I'm not being secretive. And don't do the 'boyfriend voice'. He's a friend who's a boy. Not a boyfriend. I'll see him in the next day or two, but you and Dad will probably be at work."

"Hmmm. Well, if he's here for two weeks you can surely invite him round at some point when your dad and I are here?"

"Maybe."

"At least it's someone your own age instead of you wasting your time with these mad old women."

Bet you wouldn't call them that to their faces, Callie thought.

"You know you have to put all this nonsense out of your head, Callie. It's unnatural, unhealthy. You're *not* different from everybody else. If you'd just make a bit more of an effort to fit in you'd find it easier to make friends."

Callie gritted her teeth. They'd been having this

argument over and over since Rose had started teaching her how to use her powers, and she knew that nothing she said would make any difference.

"I just want you to be happy," Julia said.

"I know."

Chutney Mary wound herself round Callie's ankles in a show of solidarity. Sometimes Callie felt as though she had more in common with the cat than with her mother.

Anna turned the car into the drive that led to East Neuk Cottages.

"Have you arranged to see Callie yet?" she asked.

"Yeah. I'm meeting her in the village this afternoon – if we manage to get the car unloaded in time."

"Don't moan. You'll be glad when you see all the food I brought. Remember trying to buy stuff at the village shop last year?"

She stopped the car in front of their cottage and went off to get the keys. Josh lounged against the bonnet, gazing at the enormous expanse of blue sky, and the duller metallic blue of the sea beyond it. They were far enough from the road to have lost the traffic noise, and apart from the sound of a tractor engine somewhere in the distance, there was only hot, blue silence.

It felt like the start of a proper holiday.

Two hours later, Josh set off to walk into the village. On the way he passed The Old Smithy, where George and Rose, Callie's grandparents, lived. Callie lived near the beach.

Josh arrived in the square, where they'd arranged to meet, and sat on a bench to wait, watching the passers-by from behind his sunglasses. After five minutes he saw a girl walking towards him. She had short, spiky brown hair and wore cut-off denim shorts, a t-shirt that was far too big for her and flip-flops. It was a few seconds before he realised it was Callie. He'd been expecting jeans and wellies and a long brown braid like last summer.

She sat down beside him and smiled at the expression on his face.

"Hello," she said.

"Hello. Wow. You look... different."

She ruffled her hair. "Yeah. Well... Thought I'd try something new."

"It's... actually, it's okay. It suits you."

"Beach?" Callie jumped up, and looked Josh up and down as he got to his feet, taking in his board shorts and Superdry tee. "Your hair's longer."

He pushed it out of his eyes. "Mum's always on at me to get it cut."

"My mum's on at me to grow mine again."

Parents. Josh and Callie grinned at each other, the ice broken, and began to meander down to the beach.

When they got there, they found the little car park above the dunes crowded with cars, and an ice-cream van parked at a precarious angle on the grass verge. They bought 99s then looked for a place away from sticky, squabbling children on the sand. Josh gave a family with an Alsatian a wide berth and he and Callie settled themselves against a hummock of red rock.

"I'd forgotten you're scared of dogs," Callie teased.

"Not *scared*. Just... cautious. They're all still wolves, I reckon, just waiting for their chance."

Josh watched the waves running in.

"I've got a body board with me, but the waves aren't really big enough," he said.

"They will be when the wind goes round to the east. It'll change in a couple of days. It's really good then – cold, though, even when the weather's like this."

"Do you want to give it a go tomorrow?"

"It'll be too calm. The next day should be better. We could go into St Andrews instead, or have you got plans?"

"No plans. It's supposed to be a holiday, but Mum's brought her laptop."

"Another book?"

Josh nodded. "Some art thing she's editing." He wondered now why he'd been nervous of seeing Callie again. Shuffling himself away from the rock, he lay down with a groan of pleasure. "I love it when it's hot. I'll have to go and live in Spain or Greece or somewhere when I leave school."

He squinted up at Callie. "Why did you cut your hair?"

She shrugged. "Fancied a change. And I thought I should give everyone at school something new to talk about." She couldn't quite keep the bleakness out of her voice.

"Ah. So you haven't suddenly got interested in the

stupid stuff that everyone else likes and made loads of friends then?"

Callie snorted. "As if." She twisted round to lie on her stomach, staring at Josh, who had his eyes closed. "If I was at school with you in Edinburgh, you'd think I was weird too. You wouldn't talk to me."

Josh opened his eyes and his mouth quickly, then stopped to think before he spoke, uncomfortably aware that there was some truth in what she had said.

"You're right. I probably wouldn't. Sorry. Back home – in school – I'd be one of the idiots who's interested in stupid stuff, and tries to look cool. It's just easier that way. Or at least, it's hard to stop once you start." He grimaced. "You probably wouldn't want to speak to me there anyway. But I don't have to worry about all that stuff here. I'm on holiday from trying to be cool. I can just be me, and you," he smiled, "you're always... you."

"You're not weird anyway," he added hastily. "You just know weird stuff. You're okay. And you fit here really well. You're part of the place." He shook his head, laughing at himself. "That sounds really stupid."

Callie was staring at him intently.

"What?" he asked.

"What if I'm weirder than you think?" Her heart was beating faster as she said it, and she felt the familiar tingling in her palms. She tried to push it down, concentrating her gaze on a pile of seaweed nearby.

Josh raised his eyebrows. "What do you mean?"

Callie saw a wisp of smoke rising from the seaweed and stared at the rock in front of her instead.

"Nothing. It doesn't matter."

✛✛✛

In St Andrews the next morning there was a queue almost to the front door of Janetta's Ice-cream Parlour, although it wasn't even ten o'clock. Josh didn't mind, though: it gave him just enough time to decide what flavours to have. Coffee. And raspberry. And a fudge finger stuck in the top.

He and Callie wandered past the cathedral ruins at ice-cream-licking speed.

"Oh no," Callie said suddenly, coming to a halt.

"What?"

"The girl walking towards us, smiling. She hates me."

"She looks friendly enough."

"Trust me, she's poison."

"Hello, Callie," said Evie, beaming. "How are you? Having a good summer?" Her eyes were fixed on Josh all the time she spoke. "Aren't you going to introduce me to your... friend?"

"Evie – Josh," Callie said, with a marked lack of enthusiasm. "Well, we'd better be off."

"I'm having a party next Friday. Why don't you both come?"

"Sorry, I can't," said Callie without hesitation.

"Well then, Josh, why don't you come on your own? Starts at eight. Callie knows the address."

"Umm... thanks."

"Must go. See you then, I hope. Your ice cream's dripped down your top, Callie."

Josh, watching Callie's expression as she stared at Evie's retreating back, half expected the other girl to spontaneously combust.

"Not one of your best mates, then?" he said.

"You could say that. She would have ignored me if you hadn't been here. Never mind her. She'll be off to have her nails permed or her hair massaged or something. What do *you* want to do?"

Josh shrugged. "Dunno. Don't mind really, only not shops."

"Not even the cake shop?" She flashed a smile.

"I'll make an exception for that. Might leave it till a bit later, though."

"We could go to the castle."

"Okay."

Callie led Josh down a narrow lane and as they emerged at the other end he saw the ruins of St Andrews Castle across the road, straight in front of him.

He started to cross, but Callie caught his arm.

"Just a minute." She pulled him a few paces from the end of the lane. "Look." She pointed at the ground.

Josh looked. She was pointing at a circular metal plate in the pavement just in front of someone's front door, like a manhole cover, but peppered with small holes.

He looked at Callie questioningly.

"What? St Andrews' most famous manhole cover?"

Callie smirked. "Just wait. It'll make sense in a bit. Come on, let's go in."

Josh paused at the gate to read the notice about ticket prices and started to fish in his pocket for money, but Callie shook her head.

"You won't need money."

Puzzled, he followed her into the entrance building.

Behind the ticket desk stood an elderly lady, watching with a gimlet eye as two tourists picked up and put down one souvenir after another. She looked as though she was trying to will them to leave, Josh thought and, just as he did so, they both put down the tea towels they'd been admiring and went out of the door at the far side of the shop.

When Josh glanced back at the ticket lady he could have sworn the smile she wore was one of triumph, but it couldn't be, of course.

"Hello, Bessie," Callie said to her.

"Good morning, dear. How are you? And this must be Josh, I suppose?"

Callie nodded. "Josh, this is Bessie Dunlop. She's a friend of Rose's."

"Hello. Nice to meet you," said Josh automatically.

"Are you going in?" Bessie asked.

"Yes, please, Bessie. I'm showing Josh the sights and it must be at least two years since I've been round the place. Does Josh have to pay?"

Bessie made a tutting noise. "Of course not, since he's with you. We can't treat him like one of these pesky tourists. They get everywhere you know, Josh, cluttering the place up. It would be much quieter without them. Still, I suppose they keep me out of mischief." She exchanged a glance with Callie that could only be described as conspiratorial, then looked round to check there were no inconvenient tourists bearing down on them. "Coast's clear. In you go."

"Thanks, Bessie. See you later."

The castle was four sides of a ruin round a central

square of daisy-spotted grass, all perched right on the cliff edge.

Josh wandered round, reading the information boards to work out what the various crumbling walls had been.

"How old is it?" he asked Callie.

"I can't remember when it was built, but it was destroyed in the sixteenth century."

"By the English?"

"No, the French. Some tourists in Pitmillie asked George about it once and when he told them about the French destroying it, they asked him what sort of aircraft they'd used."

Josh burst out laughing. "Seriously? In the sixteenth century?"

Callie nodded, grinning. "Some people just don't get history properly."

They looked over the cliff edge, trying to imagine what it must have been like to watch a fleet of ships come to destroy you.

"Come on," said Callie, pulling him away, "I want to show you something."

She led Josh to one corner of the ruin, where a flight of steps disappeared down through the grass and underground, for all the world like a giant rabbit hole.

"A dungeon?" he guessed.

Callie shook her head and stood aside to let him go first.

At the foot of the stairs was a tunnel bored into the solid rock, with a handrail on one side and lights cutting through the gloom at intervals. The roof was so low that Josh had to bend almost double.

"What *is* this place?" he asked as he shuffled along uncomfortably.

"Wait till you get to the ladder, then I'll explain," Callie said mystifyingly, creeping along behind him.

"I hope it's not far," Josh groaned as he bashed his head on the roof yet again a couple of minutes later, but just as he spoke, the top of a metal ladder came into view.

Josh climbed down the slippery treads and found, to his relief, that he could stand up properly at the bottom. He listened to water dripping from the roof as he waited for Callie to join him.

"Okay. What is this place?"

"The castle was under siege and the people outside got fed up, so they started to tunnel in under the castle wall. This is their tunnel." Callie gestured round them. "But the people *inside* found out, so *they* dug a tunnel to intercept the one coming in. The first bit – where it's really low – is that tunnel. Come on, let's go to the end."

They had to go carefully: this part of the tunnel was much wetter, trails of moisture on the walls shining in the weak light, and the floor was very slippery.

Josh reached up to the roof. The surface was velvety-soft – not at all what he had expected. When he looked at his fingers they were black, and he realised that the roof was caked with soot.

As he stretched to touch it again, a vivid picture suddenly formed in his mind, of what it must have been like down here for the men who had dug it out.

No light but guttering candles and lamps. The stink of tallow and cheap lamp oil. The noise, endlessly repeated, of picks and hammers on rock. The constant drip of water. The fear of rock falls...

"Come to the end," Callie said, breaking in on his thoughts.

The tunnel ended in a flight of stone steps that must once have led to the surface but had long since been blocked off. Above Josh's head, thin shafts of sunlight speared down into the dim tunnel in a circular pattern that looked strangely familiar.

"Recognise it?"

What was it?

He went up the steps so he could look more closely.

"The manhole cover!" he realised suddenly. "We're under the pavement across the road."

They turned to go back. The lights seemed dimmer somehow – must be because they'd been staring at the sun coming through the grating, thought Josh.

"What happened when the two tunnels met?" he asked.

"There was a battle, of course... well, a fight at any rate. I don't suppose there can have been enough people down here for a proper battle. It must have been terrible, though – no room to fight properly, nowhere to run, no escape."

Without warning, the lights went off.

4. WHISPERS IN THE DARK

Callie gasped, heard Josh beside her draw in his breath sharply. Around them was utter darkness.

"Power cut?" said Josh.

There was a pause before Callie answered. "Must be."

Their voices were swallowed by the dead air.

"Wait until I get to you," Josh said.

Callie had been at the bottom of the steps when they were plunged into darkness, but he was two – or was it three? – steps above her.

He groped forward with his feet, feeling for the edge of each step, arms outstretched, trying to find Callie.

The silence was oppressive now, no sound but the drip of water.

"Josh?" whispered Callie.

"*Here,*" whispered a voice to her left, and then, "Here," said Josh much more loudly, but on her right.

Imagination. Stop it.

"I've got my hands out. Stand still so I can find you," he went on.

Callie gave a little gasp as something touched her left wrist, and a second later Josh bumped into her from the right.

"Sorry."

"Okay." She sounded breathless.

"We can wait until the lights..."

"No!" exclaimed Callie vehemently, clutching his hand tightly. "Let's go."

They shuffled forward like cartoon zombies, arms out in front of them so they wouldn't blunder into the rock walls.

"What?" said Callie suddenly.

"What?" Josh echoed.

"You said my name."

"No I didn't," Josh insisted. Callie clutched more tightly at his hand. "You all right?" he asked.

"Fine," she said in a strained voice.

Callie.

You have come to us.

Callie stopped dead. "Did you hear that?"

"I didn't hear anything." There was a clang as Josh bumped into the ladder.

You're imagining things, Callie tried to tell herself. *Don't be stupid. There's only you and Josh down here. No one else. Nothing else.*

"Do you want to go up first?" Josh asked.

"Yes!" She couldn't keep the fear out of her voice.

Something brushed, moth-soft, against her cheek, and she failed to suppress a scream.

"Callie, what is it?"

Callie.

You are ours.

Panic overwhelmed her. She dropped Josh's hand, flailed for the cold metal of the ladder and scrambled up it, heedless of anything but the need to escape the darkness, escape the whispering voices that were suddenly all around her.

You belong with us...
We are angry...
So frightened...
Stay in the black dark with us...
Always...
We long for the light...
So much anger...
We long for the air...
We belong with you...
Callie...

"Callie!" Josh yelled. He felt for the ladder and pulled himself up.

There was a glimmer of grey here, not light, but a lessening of the darkness. He could hear Callie whimpering ahead of him, and make her out as a vague crawling shape on the floor of the passage just ahead of him. He reached forward to touch her and the lights came back on.

Blinded, he threw up his hands to shield his eyes.

"Callie, are you okay?" he asked, but there was no sound but his own voice, and when he opened his eyes properly there was no one there.

Josh hurried up the tunnel. How had Callie got out so fast, so silently? He was relieved when he emerged into air and light and saw her sitting against a wall, knees hugged to her chest, face chalky white.

"Are you okay?"

Callie nodded, hugging her knees tighter to disguise the fact that she was shaking uncontrollably. She couldn't have stood up if her life had depended on it.

"It was pretty creepy, the lights going out like that." He gave her a sideways glance, watching for some reaction. "What happened to you down there?"

Callie swallowed, unsure if her voice would work.

"Claustrophobia. I suppose I panicked."

"I didn't know you had claustrophobia."

"Neither did I."

They sat in silence for a while. Callie gradually loosened her grip on her knees. As they watched, a group of tourists reached the steps at the entrance to the mine.

"They won't get far in the dark," Callie said, still sounding a bit odd.

"But the lights came on again – remember? When you were crawling out of the top bit."

"No they didn't. It was still dark when I got out." She gave a shaky laugh. "And I certainly wasn't crawling. I was running as fast as I could."

She's confused, Josh told himself. *She was so frightened back there she doesn't remember what she did.*

Callie had unlaced her hands from around her knees now, and was rubbing at her sooty left hand and wrist.

"Let's get out of here," she said, getting to her feet.

"Should we tell Mrs Dunlop about the lights?" Josh wondered aloud.

Callie shook her head. "Let's just go. You said they came back on. Someone else can tell her if they go off again."

Back on the street, Josh would have liked to pause and look at the circular grating again, but Callie kept up a determined pace and ignored it.

"Do you want to have a walk round the cathedral?" he asked.

"No," said Callie firmly. "I've had enough of ruins for today."

"Fudge doughnut?"

"Much better idea."

By the time they had eaten the doughnuts and licked the last of the custard off their fingers, Callie seemed, outwardly at least, back to normal.

"What time is it?"

Josh checked his phone. "Nearly one."

"Rats! I've got to go. I promised George I'd go down to Fife Ness with him this afternoon. You know – the place on the coast where he's got his birdwatching patch. He wants help with some birding thing. Dunno what, but I'll have to get the next bus to The Smithy. Do you want to come? You probably don't, it won't be very exciting. You'd be better staying in town."

"No, I'll come. I like George. He's cool."

"You must be joking."

"No, he is. He knows lots of stuff. About birds for instance, and plants. I don't know anybody in Edinburgh who knows things like that. It's interesting."

Callie laughed. "Wait until I tell him he's cool. He'll love that."

As they walked through The Smithy garden, Josh said, "Are you sure they won't mind me just turning up for lunch?"

"Course not." She shoved open the front door and Luath came to greet them, wagging his plume of a tail. "He still remembers you, or he'd bark."

Josh tried to remind himself how friendly Luath was, instead of noticing afresh how big he was.

"Rose? George? I brought Josh for lunch."

"Oh well done, dear. I wondered when we'd see him," said Rose, appearing, inevitably, from the kitchen. "Goodness, why are you both so grubby? You look as though you've been down a tunnel. Why are you laughing?"

Josh ate so much of Rose's chicken pie and strawberry fool that he could hardly bear to get out of the car at Fife Ness.

"Come on, you pig," Callie teased as he levered himself up with a groan. "Or shall I see if I can borrow a golf trolley to push you round on?"

"Yes, please," he said, squinting into the sunlight at the golf course off to their left. "If a golf ball comes this way and hits me, I might just explode."

"Exercise, that's what you need," said George.

Josh doubted it, but he dutifully followed George and Callie.

"Right," said George, opening the holdall he'd been carrying. "Hatchet or saw?" He held them up for Josh to inspect.

"Er... hatchet please. I think. What are we doing?"

"Stalking holidaymakers," said Callie with an evil grin.

"Not quite that exciting," said George, handing another hatchet to Callie and keeping the saw himself. "Cutting branches that are in my way when I'm trying to ring birds. It's all right, I'll show you what to do."

It was hot work, hacking away at the gorse and scrubby trees that George wanted trimmed. Stopping to mop her brow, Callie noticed a sooty mark on her left wrist. She rubbed at it, but it wouldn't come off.

Witch-girl...

She whirled round to see who had spoken, but there was no one there. She could hear George and Josh on the other side of a huge gorse bush, laughing, but the voice had come from the opposite direction. She swallowed, holding tightly to the hatchet, looking about as if she expected someone to leap out of the undergrowth.

"Callie!"

She jumped at the sound of Josh's voice.

"What?"

"You must be slacking. We can't hear you chopping."

"Just having a quick rest." She shook her head at her overactive imagination, and started hacking away at branches again.

Half an hour later, the trimming was finished to George's satisfaction and he was settling down in the shade with his binoculars to see which birds were around.

Josh and Callie wandered off along the shore. Unlike Pitmillie beach, it was almost deserted.

"Wind's going round," Callie observed. "Should be good for body boarding tomorrow if you still fancy it?"

"Definitely."

After half an hour or so they made their way back to George's birdwatching patch and found him finishing a mug of tea.

"Nothing around. Too hot, I expect. They'll all be lying low in the shade," he said with regret. "We may as well go, but we'll go back by Dane's Dyke just in case there are any birds around there."

"George, tell Josh the story. The one you used to tell me when I was small."

"The one I regretted telling you, you mean."

"What story?" asked Josh.

"It's not a story really, Callie, it's local history," George corrected her. As they walked on, he began to talk.

"Long ago, the Danes came raiding in Fife over and over, and there's supposed to have been a great battle here in eight hundred and eighty something. I forget the exact date. It's not very clear what happened: either they won and killed King Constantine of Scotland, or they didn't win and they didn't kill him. Nobody seems to know either way." He led them up onto a grassy bank about a metre high. "Anyway, you're standing on what's been known as Dane's Dyke ever since."

From the name, Josh would have expected something impressive: a wall maybe, or a defensive earthwork at least a couple of metres high. The bank they stood on was covered in grass and scrubby weeds. It stretched off in a gentle curve, getting lower and lower until it merged with the ground around it.

It really wasn't that interesting. However, he didn't want to seem rude, so...

"What is it? Was it some sort of defence?"

George beamed. "Everyone assumed so, but it turns out it's more than that. There was some excavation done a few years ago, and it turned up human bones."

"It's a grave?" *That* was more interesting.

"It seems to be – or part of it is, anyway."

"He hasn't told you the best bit," Callie said. "Go on George. Josh won't think you're nuts. He already knows there's more to this part of Fife than meets the eye."

Now Josh was *really* intrigued.

George hesitated for a few seconds, then started to speak again.

"When I was a couple of years older than you I used to come birdwatching down here with an old chap called John Fordyce who'd lived in Crail all his life. One day he took me along Dane's Dyke, right to the far end." George pointed towards the sea. "Up at the top of the bank he showed me a big stone slab. He levered it up and there was a human skeleton underneath.

"Well, you can imagine what went through my mind; I thought I was being shown the scene of a murder at first. Then I looked at the bones properly and realised they must be pretty old. They were dark brown, some of them were broken into fragments. Even to me, it was obvious they must have been there for a very long time.

"John Fordyce called the place The Longman's Grave, said it was where a great Danish warrior was buried. The Longman had sworn to protect his men, and the legend was that he did so even after they were dead, to stop them roaming the earth as ghosts. John claimed the Longman still took – what was it he called them now – *the unquiet dead*, that was it – down to the underworld occasionally, to keep our world safe from them.

"I asked my parents about the grave as soon as I went home. They'd come across the name, of course – you can find that on maps – but they'd never heard of there actually being a grave there."

"Can we go and have a look now?" asked Josh eagerly.

"No," said George. "That's the strange thing. I was never able to find the grave again. Not a sign. I've looked for it on and off for years. There are references to Longman's Grave in a few books, but nothing about a slab or a skeleton. I know what I saw, but I stopped talking about it to other people after a while, because I could see they didn't believe me. They thought I was just making it up."

"Why didn't you ask John Fordyce?"

"It was a few weeks before I got the chance to look for the grave again, and he'd died in the meantime."

"But I thought you said bones had been found in the dyke a few years ago?" Josh said, confused.

"Yes, but that was at the other end," Callie replied.

The bank had been getting lower as they walked and now it petered out, merging into the landscape.

"I've looked too," said Callie.

"I used to wish I'd never told you the story, you pestered me about it that much when you were small," said George ruefully. "Anyway, Josh, if you're thinking of going digging for it yourself, it'll have to be another day – I'll need to be getting back now."

+++

"Anybody home?" Callie yelled as she went into her own house.

"Just me," replied her father, David, his voice coming from the back garden.

She found him sitting in the sun with the newspaper, a cup of coffee and a packet of biscuits.

"Had a nice day?" he asked.

"Yeah. Just mucking about with Josh." She shoved a biscuit into her mouth. "We're going body boarding tomorrow, but I don't think he's realised how cold it'll be. Can I lend him your wetsuit?"

"Will it fit?"

"It'll be better than no wetsuit at all. And he's only a few centimetres shorter than you."

"No problem."

"Where's Mum?"

"Gone to see your grandmother." He looked at her questioningly. "Is there something going on with them? It seems a bit... tense... these days."

Callie knew that her father was a clever man, but he could be *very* slow to notice things going on in front of his nose sometimes.

She shrugged. "Dunno," she said evasively. "When's tea? I'm going for a shower."

"In about an hour. I'm on barbecue duty."

"Cool. Will there be prawns?"

"Of course."

"Yum."

Callie was glad to get into the shower. She still felt

grubby and gritty from this morning's episode at the castle. It was strange just how spooked she'd been when the lights went out, imagining all that stuff. It seemed ridiculous now; Josh must have thought she was crazy. She pushed away the memory of the voice at Fife Ness.

The black mark on her left wrist wouldn't come off, no matter how hard she rubbed. Odd. It wasn't a graze, and it was the wrong colour for a bruise. It looked almost as if some soot had got under her skin. It was an unwelcome reminder of what had happened earlier in the day, and when she got dressed again she pulled her sleeve down to cover it so that her parents wouldn't notice and ask about it.

There were prawns, and tuna and sausages too. And corn on the cob. And bananas with chocolate in them. They always made too much when they had a barbecue.

"You should have invited Josh over," said David, looking at the leftovers.

"He's going out somewhere with his mum," Callie replied quickly.

"At least we can say hello to him tomorrow if he's coming in to borrow your dad's wetsuit," said Julia. "Have you dug it out for him yet, David?"

"Not yet, but I haven't forgotten," said David, basking, eyes closed, in a patch of sunlight.

"You will bring him in to meet us, won't you? Your grandparents have seen him today. Now it's our turn," Julia pressed on.

55

"All right. I'll bring him in." It was probably best just to get it over with.

Julia beamed.

It was a warm night. Another warm night. Callie slid the bedroom window up a few more centimetres, but the wind had dropped completely and now there wasn't even enough breeze to stir the curtains. Chutney Mary lay on the bed in a purring heap.

"Don't dare snuggle up to me, cat. If you make me too hot I'm shutting you out for the night," Callie warned her as she climbed into bed, pushing the cat to one side. Chutney Mary gave a chirp of protest and settled down again as Callie opened a book.

Deep in the night, the cat woke suddenly, ears pricked, alert. At this time of year the sky never seemed to be totally dark, and there was enough light for her eyes.

She watched her mistress, quietly asleep, covers flung back because of the heat, then her eyes narrowed at something: a tiny, hunched, formless blot of darkness that moved across the bed. The cat's ears went back as the darkness drifted to the floor, and settled, and slipped down through a narrow gap between the floorboards.

Chutney Mary hissed.

5. BAD DREAM

The doorbell rang. Callie hurried to answer it before her mother. "Come in," she said to Josh.

He propped his body board against the wall just inside the gate and slid his bag off his shoulders.

"Waves look good," he said. "I thought when the wind dropped last night it was going to be rubbish, but it's back up this morning."

Callie yawned.

"Late night?" Josh asked.

She shook her head. "Weird dreams."

"Weird how?"

She found she didn't want to talk about her dreams. They had been oddly disturbing. *Don't be so stupid,* she told herself. *They were only dreams.* "People whispering to me." She felt her palms itch. "Lots of hammering. I must have been building a wall or something."

Without warning, the gate swung open behind Josh and banged shut, making them both jump.

"Er... Callie... you don't use a hammer to build a wall," Josh said, eyeing the gate suspiciously.

"Knocking it down then. Whatever. I'll get the suit," said Callie, keen to change the subject.

"Callie, is that Josh?" her mother's voice called from upstairs.

"Yes," Callie yelled back. "She wants to meet you," she said to Josh, making a face.

"I'd quite like to meet her. And your dad."

"Really?" Callie looked astonished. "Go into the kitchen and have a seat while I get the wetsuit."

"It's really warm out there, though."

She laughed. "There speaks someone who's never been in the sea in Fife."

Callie, going out, almost collided with Julia, coming in. "Back in a minute," Callie said, continuing determinedly on her way.

The wetsuits were hanging in the garage where Callie's father was tinkering with his ancient and beloved Morris Traveller car. Callie took down her own and her dad's.

"I take it Josh has arrived?"

"Yeah. Mum's got him cornered in the kitchen."

"Now, now. She's just interested. We don't often get to meet your friends. And this must be quite a friendship to have kept going when you've seen so little of each other."

Callie thought about that and nodded. "I suppose it is. Are you coming in to meet him too?"

"Am I allowed to?"

"Ha ha."

When they got back to the kitchen they found Josh chatting to Julia without looking in the least bit cornered, but Callie was itching to go, and after giving her dad a brief chance to say hello she dragged Josh away.

"At least that's over," she said grimly as she shut the gate behind them.

"You make it sound like some sort of torture," Josh laughed.

"It was for me."

They started to walk down the beach road.

"Dunno why. They seem okay."

"It's just they – well, Mum really – always want to know what I'm doing, and why I'm not hanging out with other people. And she disapproves of some of the stuff I do and just goes on and on about it."

Josh couldn't imagine Callie doing anything much that a parent would disapprove of.

"What sort of stuff?"

Oh, just the usual sort of witchy stuff: conjuring lights, talking through water, casting the net to protect things. I did mention I'm a witch, didn't I?

"Just stuff. Never mind – it's too good a day to waste it talking about parents."

The waves were as good as Callie had predicted and they spent a couple of hours messing about in the surf before hunger pulled them back to the beach and the picnic lunch they'd brought.

"Okay," said Josh, round a mouthful of sandwich. "You were right. I'd have been frozen without the wetsuit. You never know, I could have been the first person in Scotland to get sunstroke and hypothermia simultaneously if it wasn't for you."

"Told you so," Callie said with a triumphant smirk as she rummaged in the bag for a drink. "You just need to learn to accept that I'm always right."

"What did you do to your wrist?" Josh asked, pointing to the mark on Callie's arm.

"Dunno. Nothing," she said, quickly pulling the sleeve of her sweatshirt down to cover it and forcing herself to be calm so that the tingling in her fingers would go.

Josh grabbed the can out of her hand, shook it and tore back the ring-pull so that it squirted in her face.

Callie shrieked. "Right, you... you... This is war." And she chased him back into the waves.

"Let me drop off the wetsuits and I'll walk up with you," said Callie. "I've got to go over to The Smithy."

Callie disappeared into her house without asking Josh in, so he leaned against the wall and tried to pull his fingers through his salt-stiff hair. He wondered why she was so neurotic about her parents. They seemed okay: not especially embarrassing, no more so than his own mother.

The sound of the front door slamming cut across his thoughts and Callie reappeared beside him.

There were three cars parked outside The Smithy when they reached it.

"They must have visitors," said Josh.

"It's just Rose's friends," said Callie.

Another few steps and he could see over the gate and into the garden, where Rose, Bessie and another two elderly ladies sat in deckchairs sunning themselves like cats around a table laden with tea and cakes. Luath sprawled on the grass nearby looking like a melted dog.

"Pour me another cuppa, would you, Bessie?" one of them said.

Josh realised he must have been out in the sun for too long because he thought, for a fraction of a second, that Bessie had waved a finger and the teapot had floated up into the air on its own. He blinked hard and when he opened his eyes again, Bessie was holding the pot quite normally and waving to him and Callie.

"They're expecting you?"

"Yes. They're... sort of... tutoring me."

Josh blew out a breath. "During the holidays? That's a bit heavy. What are they tutoring you in?"

There was a very long pause.

"Local... historical stuff." Callie opened the gate. "Look, I've got to go. I'll call you tomorrow."

"Okay. Bye." Josh took one last long look at the group in the garden then turned towards East Neuk Cottages. *Local history?* Josh had no idea what was going on, but he was sure it wasn't that.

"You should have brought him in to meet Isobel and Barbara, dear," said Bessie. "He seemed a nice boy when I met him at the castle."

"He was in a rush," Callie said firmly.

The mention of the castle made her wonder if she should tell Rose about what had happened in the tunnel. She imagined how it was going to sound here in the sun, in the familiar surroundings of The Smithy, and decided against it. She'd just come across like an over-imaginative idiot.

"It's a shame he didn't come in," said Barbara. "Isobel and I won't get another chance to see him. We're both off on holiday tomorrow."

"Your mother was here yesterday," said Rose gloomily. "She says I'm ruining your life."

"No you're not," said Callie indignantly. "You're trying to help. But you know how I feel: I just want to be me; I don't want all this witch stuff. It's just going to get in the way."

"But the 'witch stuff' *is* you. It's part of you, Callie," said Isobel. "It's not going to go away."

"And it's not a *bad* thing," added Barbara. "Once you know what you're doing, it doesn't have to get in the way of anything; it can be really useful."

They'd been over this again and again, but no one seemed to have made any progress convincing Callie. On the other hand, Julia hadn't persuaded her to abandon the training either...

"Let's get started," said Bessie.

"Yes," said Rose. "Barbara, you go into the bathroom." As Barbara went, Rose filled the washing-up bowl with water. "Just you come over to the sink, Callie."

This was one of the things Callie was getting the hang of. She waited for the water surface to grow completely still, then breathed on it, saying the words of the spell in her head. The water turned hazy white, then cleared to show Barbara's face.

"Hello, Callie. Well done."

"Hello, Barbara. Can you hear me?"

"Loud and clear, dear."

"You've got this nicely, Callie." Rose was smiling now.

"You're right. This isn't hard once you get the hang of it. I suppose it's a bit like Skype, really. But I can't see the point of it. Why would you muck about with bowls of water when there's phones and texts and emails and stuff?"

Bessie harrumphed. "You don't think all that's been around for ever, do you? Anyway, just consider what happens to the lights and the radio sometimes when you're practising. Strong magic can scramble all this electrical gubbins. There'll come a time when you'll be grateful for this old-fashioned stuff. And this," she gesticulated at the bowl, "is what witches do."

Callie wasn't convinced. "When can I learn a spell that might actually be useful for something? Teach me how to stop the magic breaking out when I don't want it to. Show me how to stop my fingers tingling then something crazy happening that I didn't mean to do. If I'm stuck with witchcraft, I want to be in charge of it."

"That's all part of taking control of your power fully," said Rose. "It'll come. Surely you've noticed that it's getting better?"

"I suppose so. But it still gets away from me sometimes."

Rose gave her a sympathetic smile. "Cast the net." She handed Callie two candles.

"And you can't say this isn't useful," said Bessie, still intent on defending traditional witchcraft. "It's a spell of protection. No dark magic can cross the net."

"We think it's time you tried this on something alive," Isobel said.

"No!" Callie exclaimed instantly. "What if I get it wrong?"

"No harm done."

"No harm? Remember what happened to Bessie's teapot? I don't want to lop someone's arm off," she continued, panic-stricken.

"No, no. Not one of *us*," Isobel said.

"Luath?"

"Certainly not! I thought we'd try with something in the garden first and see if that's still in one piece when you finish with it."

"A *plant*? I thought you said something alive?"

"For goodness sake, girl. Plants are alive. You do biology, don't you?"

They trooped into the back garden, where they wouldn't be seen from the road. Rose pointed to an apple tree.

"That should do."

"George won't be pleased if I knock that down by accident," said Callie doubtfully.

"Well, he'll just have to deal with it if you do. But you won't. I wouldn't be suggesting this if I didn't think you were ready."

"All right." Callie chose her spot and set the candles down next to a rose bush covered in white blooms. Rose, Bessie, Isobel and Barbara moved to stand (safely) behind her.

Callie took a few seconds to collect her thoughts, then set fire to the wicks with a word. She spun the flames into filaments, drawing them out, twisting them into the net of light, weaving in the protective spells so that nothing could get through the net to harm what was inside.

It was ready. She took a slow breath and moved her hands to cast the net.

It floated up from her fingers, a mesh of sparkling threads. Up and over the apple tree it went, then settled around it like a veil and dissolved into shimmering mist, then into nothing.

"Oh, well done," said Barbara.

"Beautiful, dear. Couldn't have done better myself," added Isobel.

Callie looked at the tree. Not a leaf or a twig had moved. George's tree was safe. She really had done it! She was fizzing with pleasure at her achievement.

"I might even let you back into my kitchen in the future," said Bessie dryly. "You've got the basics now. We'll be able to move on to interesting stuff soon."

"I thought we were nearly finished." Callie was dismayed.

"Heavens, no," said Rose. "We've barely begun."

The white roses next to Callie shrivelled, turned brown, and fell off.

Callie trudged home. She'd been so elated when she'd managed to cast the net over the tree. She'd really thought that she'd done it, passed some sort of test, and she wouldn't have to keep thinking about being a witch any more. But now she had to start all over again, or at least that was what it felt like.

Home again, she went straight upstairs for a shower. When she went into her bedroom afterwards, she found Julia sitting on the bed.

"Why are you in my room?" she said, rubbing her hair dry with a towel.

"How long are you going to keep this nonsense up?"

"What nonsense?" Callie asked, choosing not to understand.

"You should be spending more time with Josh and your other friends, not that coven of old women."

"Coven? Surely that's what you call witches, Mother?"

"Don't get smart. I don't want you going round there again, do you understand?"

"You're trying to forbid me to visit my *grandparents*?" Callie's voice rose.

"Yes. Only until you get this ridiculous delusion out of your head."

"*Delusion*? You think this is a delusion?" Callie yelled. There was a noise like a gunshot.

Julia and Callie turned to the window. One of the panes had cracked from top to bottom.

"What have you done?" Julia hissed.

"I can't have done anything," Callie spat back. "It's a delusion, remember?"

There was a shout from downstairs. "Is everything all right up there?"

"Yes, David," Julia called, getting up. "I mean it," she said to Callie on her way out. "Keep away from The Smithy."

Callie didn't even bother to answer.

+++

Callie couldn't sleep. Chutney Mary was off hunting somewhere, and she missed the cat's comforting purr. She was upset, too, about what had happened earlier. Her window was temporarily held together with tape, and her dad had chosen to accept her claim that the pane had just cracked without anyone doing anything to cause it, but she shouldn't have let things get out of control like that. After all that Rose had said...

She punched her pillow into a comfortable position, closed her eyes.

She slept, trapped in a dream of cold and dark and stone; whispers and muttered curses, the harsh noise of hammers and picks on rock, the smell of sweat and fear. She'd been down here in the dark for ever, in the cold, surrounded by fear.

As she slept, she scratched at the mark on her wrist.

A pool of darkness seeped from the gap in the boards by Callie's bed and oozed out across the floor, slow as oil, so black it seemed to suck the last of the dim light from the room. She muttered something and tossed in her sleep, trying to break free of the dream, of the noise of hammers and pickaxes.

The floor was covered now, the bed afloat on an oily pool of something blacker than mere darkness.

Callie woke with a gasp, tangled in the bedclothes. She was blind, nothing but the black dark around her.

Out of the silence came a sound. The sound of hammer on stone. Callie froze, breath held tight.

Crack!

And again, *Crack!*

And again.

Impossible. It was the noise from her dream. She must still have been asleep.

The noise was all around her now. All around. Inside the walls of her room, under the floor, in the roof.

She wasn't asleep.

Callie screamed. She scrabbled for the switch of her bedside lamp.

Light.

The noise stopped.

"Callie, what is it?" The door flew open and her parents hurried into the room, switching on the main light. No one noticed the last fingers of darkness slipping down between the boards again.

"Did you hear it? Did you hear it? What's happening?" Callie gibbered.

"Hear what, love?" Julia asked, putting an arm round her shaking daughter. "We heard you scream, that's all."

"You've had a bad dream, that's all, Callie. You're okay now," said David.

"No! I mean, I *was* dreaming, but then I woke up and it was dark, but really, really dark, and then the noise from my dream started up again. You *must* have heard it – hammering in the walls."

Julia and David listened to Callie's half-hysterical monologue, and tried to reassure her.

"You only thought you woke up. You were still asleep. The noise in the walls was part of the dream too," Julia told her.

"No – I was awake. I'm sure of it."

"Callie, you couldn't have been. If there had been hammering, we'd have heard it. It's just your imagination working overtime."

They must be right. She must have still been asleep.

Chutney Mary chose that moment to saunter in, jump onto the bed, and present Callie with a dead mouse.

"Lovely," observed Julia.

The cat purred proudly and head-butted Callie, and as though a switch had been flicked, everything seemed normal again.

"I'm okay now," Callie said. "Sorry I woke you." She picked the mouse up by its tail and dropped it out of the window.

"Sure?"

Callie nodded. "I'll read for a bit before I go back to sleep, but I'm fine now, honestly. It was just a really vivid dream."

"Goodnight then."

"Goodnight."

6. GREY DAY

Callie woke to the sound of shouting. For a few seconds she thought she was dreaming again, then she made out her parents' voices, arguing about something.

They did argue, sometimes, but she'd never heard them shouting like that. She couldn't make out the words. Could they be arguing about her? Had her dad found out what she was?

She didn't want to go downstairs into the middle of it. Just as she was wondering whether she ought to, she heard the front door slam and there was silence. One of them had left for work.

Callie pulled the curtains open, but she wasn't quite quick enough to see who had gone.

It was a chilly grey morning: east coast weather. The haar had drifted in overnight, but she'd been expecting that, and she knew it wouldn't be gone until the afternoon. The weather seldom surprised her now; there seemed to be some special new witch-sense she'd acquired that gave her a pretty good idea of what was coming in the next day or so. One useful thing, anyway.

Josh was going to Falkland Palace with his mum, so Callie was at a loose end. She would usually have thought about scrounging lunch at The Smithy, but maybe, after the argument yesterday, she'd give that a miss for today.

She kicked off the covers. The cat had long since squirmed out of the window, a busy day of cat business ahead of her. Callie got up and took a couple of steps, then stopped and looked at the floor. The boards were covered with a thin layer of gritty grey dust. She looked more carefully, and saw that it seemed to cover the entire floor.

At once she was transported back to that awful dream. She'd been digging... Had she somehow made part of the dream real?

She pulled the curtains open and switched on the light. The floor was covered with a substance closer to grit than to dust. Something else caught Callie's attention. On the wall opposite the window was a stain. She walked across the crunchy floor to look at it more closely, touched it and found that the wall was damp. The stain extended from waist height down to the floor, a hand span wide.

What was happening? She'd thought she was getting a grip on this treacherous power, but she'd been wrong, and here was the proof.

She had to get rid of this before her mother saw it.

In the kitchen, Julia was loading the dishwasher.

"I'll do that," said Callie as she came in.

"Thanks, love." Julia straightened up, pushing her hair behind her ears.

"What were you and Dad arguing about?" Callie asked, not quite meeting her mother's eyes.

Julia sighed. "You know, I'm not really sure. It just

blew up out of nothing. I don't understand – you know we're not usually like that. Don't worry; it'll all be forgotten by tonight."

A few minutes later she was gone. Callie turned on the television and ate a banana, watching some programme without taking in anything about it. She gave up and switched it off, took a dustpan and brush upstairs and swept up the grit, then opened her window wide.

On most days this summer, that would have let in enough warmth to dry up the damp patch, but the air was dank and chilly, although it was ten in the morning.

"Hairdryer," she muttered to herself.

Half an hour later, the mark was almost gone. Callie looked round her room and decided it looked like usual. She sat down on the bed with a thump. What if her mother had been right all along about being a witch? What if she was making life more difficult for herself by learning how to use her power? Maybe, in spite of what Rose and her friends said, things would go back to normal and it would fade away if she just ignored it.

After all, she didn't really know why the old women wanted her to start using her power. It might be for their benefit, not hers. Maybe they wanted to recruit her to their coven because she was young and powerful and their abilities were fading with age.

They were using her. That was it. They wanted her fresh power for themselves. Why hadn't she seen it sooner? She must be more careful about trusting people. There weren't many you could completely trust.

Maybe there were none.

She glanced at her alarm clock and saw to her

astonishment that it was almost noon. That couldn't be right, surely? She'd sat down here a few minutes ago and it had only been half past ten. She realised she'd been rubbing at the mark on her wrist again and stopped, abruptly.

When Callie checked her phone it really was almost noon. She couldn't believe she'd been sitting there for an hour and a half: it had only felt like a few minutes.

She needed to get out of the house.

Callie dressed quickly and shut the front door behind her with a sense of relief. Right; she wanted a change of scene. She didn't want to have to think about witchcraft or secrets or grumpy parents. There was no point going to the beach on such a grey day, so she set off to catch the bus to St Andrews. By the time it arrived she'd decided to go and see the new Pixar film at the cinema. Perfect – she'd revert to being a kid for the afternoon and go back to a time before life got so stupidly complicated.

As she sat on the bus, the mark on her wrist itched. She rubbed at it, still puzzled as to what it was. Looking at it, she thought it seemed bigger than she remembered, and peered more closely, but she was no nearer to working out why it wouldn't come off or what it could be. Maybe Rose would know.

Callie felt a pang as she recalled the crazy things she'd been imagining about Rose and the rest of the coven that morning. She *knew* they were trying to look after her – what on earth had she been thinking? She was ashamed of herself.

+++

Of course, the cinema was crammed with damp families escaping the haar, popcorn crunching underfoot like biodegradable gravel, but the film was bright and funny and Callie was in a good mood when she got off the bus in Pitmillie. She felt that her mind was her own again.

She had wondered briefly whether to tell Rose about what had been happening, but decided not to. Surely she ought to be able to deal with it herself? After all, this was *her* power and *her* problem. She wanted to solve it without everyone watching her.

No one was in when she got home, not even the cat. Callie checked her room and found, to her relief, that everything looked all right. In an effort to stay busy she examined the contents of the fridge, looking for clues to what supper was meant to be, and started to cook. It would be worth it just to see the look of astonishment on her mother's face, she thought, as she chopped onions. And whatever had been intended, supper was definitely curry now.

When everything was bubbling away and the kitchen was full of the scents of spices, Callie went for a shower. The sun had broken through at last, and the upstairs of the house was flooded with light. She sensed the weather would be back to warm and sunny tomorrow.

She took her phone into the bathroom so she could listen to music and sang along happily in the shower until the moment when the water suddenly ran freezing cold. She leapt back with a scream.

"Stupid shower! Behave!" She turned the temperature control down then back up and stuck her hand cautiously into the water. Back to normal.

When it happened for a second and then a third time, she gave up. The thermostat must have gone or something.

She got dressed, went to check on the curry, and found the kitchen filled with steam and the hot tap full on.

Callie turned off the tap and stared at it. She must have turned it on without realising. At least it explained where all the hot water had disappeared to.

She knew it wasn't quite enough of an explanation, but she was determined not to think about it too much.

"Who are you and what have you done with my daughter?"

Callie gave a gasp and spun round to find her mother looking at the bubbling pots in astonishment.

"Don't do that! You gave me a fright."

"It's amazing. You look like Callie, you sound like Callie – but you can cook."

"Oh, ha ha. Very funny. If that's the thanks I get for trying to be helpful..."

"It's just the shock. I *am* grateful, honestly. You should do it more often." Julia paused. "You *should* do it more often, you know. You're in before Dad or me quite a lot, but it's always me who has to cook."

"Schoolwork? Remember? I'm meant to study."

"You usually seem to be studying Facebook or iTunes when I get in."

Callie opened her mouth to protest, but Julia held up her hands with a grimace.

"Sorry. Sorry. I don't know why I reacted like that. Can we start again? Thanks for cooking. It smells really good."

"No problem," Callie replied a bit stiffly.

"When will it be ready?"

"About twenty minutes," said Callie, distracted by a new text on her phone.

"Perfect."

"I'm going over to the cottages to hang out with Josh this evening," she said once she'd read it.

"Okay."

Josh and Callie floated on their backs in the tiny octagonal swimming pool at East Neuk Cottages, trying to move as little as possible but still stay afloat.

"How was Falkland?"

"Meh... I suppose it's quite nice as palaces go. I liked the tennis court; you know, it's one of those crazy old ones where you have to hit the ball off the roof or something..."

"Royal Tennis?"

"Yeah... that's it. And Mum was raving about the gardens. I suppose they were quite pretty."

"Mmnn... George likes them too."

"That reminds me – how did your history tutorial go?"

"My what?" Callie lifted her head clear of the water, wondering what on earth Josh meant.

"Yesterday. With Rose and her friends."

Callie let her feet sink to the floor of the pool and pushed herself upright.

"Oh, that," she said, suddenly remembering the lie she had told him. "Fine." She swam over to the side and looked out of the window and across the field to The Smithy. *Should I tell him about what's been happening at home? It's so tempting... But he'll think I'm more than weird if I tell him. That'll probably be the end of our friendship, and I need a friend right now.*

"So what did you learn?"

"Just... bits and pieces. Nothing really interesting."

There is something, Josh thought, *that Callie isn't telling me. She's distracted, preoccupied. What's going on between her and Rose's friends?*

He was sure it was something more interesting than local history. Maybe she'd be more talkative out of the water.

"Do you fancy some chocolate cake?" he asked.

Callie hadn't realised they would have to make the chocolate cake themselves before they could eat it.

"I didn't know you could bake," she said as she licked cake mixture off a finger.

Josh raised his eyebrows. "What, you think guys can't bake? That's a bit sexist."

"No, of course... well, I suppose I did mean that, sort of."

Josh shook his head in mock disgust. "For that, you have to wash-up. Honestly, you country people, you're practically prehistoric."

Three games of pool, one DVD and half a chocolate cake later, Callie set off for home, having arranged to spend the next day at the beach with Josh and successfully defeated his attempts to find out more about the "tutorials".

It still wasn't properly dark when she got home, although it was nearly eleven o'clock.

"Hello, Callie," said her dad. "Good time?"

"Yeah. I beat Josh at pool." She yawned. "I'm going up to bed. Still tired after last night."

"Let's hope there are no nightmares tonight, then," said Julia.

"Hope not. Goodnight."

Callie pushed her bedroom door open cautiously, unsure what to expect. It all looked normal. Chutney Mary had already come in through the window and was curled up snoozing at the foot of the bed.

Maybe whatever had happened last night had been a one-off, a sort of waking nightmare.

Callie was woken from a deep sleep by the sound of the cat hissing. Half asleep, it took her a few seconds to realise what the noise was.

"What is it, puss?" she muttered groggily.

Chutney Mary was perched at the end of the bed, staring fixedly at a point under Callie's desk. Every muscle in her body was taut and the fur on her tail stuck out like a bottle brush.

Callie was suddenly very wide awake, adrenalin surging in her blood. *What is the cat staring at?*

There was some moonlight coming in through the half-open curtains, so the room wasn't particularly dark, but under the desk was a pool of total blackness.

Very slowly, Callie reached out to turn on her bedside light. It gave out a wan glow, quite unlike its usual self, that barely reached the end of the bed. The pool of darkness beneath the desk remained utterly unilluminated, and the cat continued to hiss.

Fighting down fear, Callie sat up properly and moved slowly forward until she was kneeling beside the cat. From here, the darkness looked solid, three dimensional, squatting malevolently on the floor. If Callie looked straight at it, it seemed to blur and waver, as though she was seeing it through a heat haze.

Tap.

Tap. Tap.

The hair stood up on Callie's neck.

Crack!

The sound of hammer on stone, coming from under the floor, from under the bed where she knelt.

Too frightened to move, she tried desperately to remember one of the spells of protection that Rose had been teaching her, but all the words had fled.

The noise was all around now, coming from the floor, the walls, the ceiling... Why could no one else hear it?

Beside her the cat gave a tremulous yowl and rose to her feet, stiff-legged. Callie followed her gaze and saw to her horror a figure uncoiling itself from the blackness under the desk, arms reaching up...

7. CONFESSION

A dark figure reared up into the room as Callie shrank back in terror.

"What on earth are you doing to the cat?"

The door opened, the main light went on and, inexplicably, her father spoke into silence. Where the figure had been there was only the floor and the desk and the wall.

"Callie? What are you doing? It's two in the morning."

"I'm... What? I'm..."

"Did you have another nightmare?"

"No... I... I don't know."

Chutney Mary was sitting on the bed licking her paws as though nothing had happened. Callie tried to collect what was left of her mind.

"What did you do to the cat?" her father asked again.

"Nothing. She woke me up hissing. What woke you?"

"The noise the cat was making, of course. Why? Did you hear things again?"

"No. No," said Callie firmly. "Just the cat."

"Put her out and shut the window so she can't get back in."

"No. I'm sure she'll be quiet now."

"She'd better be, or I'll put her out myself. Goodnight."

David shut the door.

For a few minutes, Callie stared at the perfectly ordinary, unthreatening space under the desk, then she glanced at the cat, who was already asleep again.

"Unbelievable," she muttered, and tiptoed over to the desk to check it properly.

There was no sign that anything out of the ordinary had just happened, but this time Callie had no doubts that it had.

She marshalled her thoughts and whispered the words of a spell of protection under her breath, then checked every inch of the room before getting back into bed. She couldn't stop looking at the desk, but with the main light and the bedside lamp on there wasn't even a scrap of shadow underneath it.

All the same, Callie kept an eye on it. She didn't understand how the cat could go straight back to sleep, but it must be a good sign, surely? Chutney Mary seemed to have some sort of radar for whatever was happening, and it clearly wasn't picking anything up just now. Callie was somewhat reassured by that, but not nearly enough to even consider going back to sleep. She settled down to wait for morning.

The cat was tramping back and forward across her chest to wake her. *To wake her.* That meant she must have fallen asleep. How could she have slept? And yet, looking back now, the frightening events of the night were hazy in her memory. She couldn't have been dreaming. She couldn't have. Could she?

Perhaps she should tell Rose, but there was something she needed to try first. She didn't know why she hadn't thought of it sooner.

Callie fumbled for her alarm clock. Eight thirty. The house was silent: both her parents would already have left for work.

She decided not to bother with a shower. After all, she'd be in and out of the sea later, and she had more important things to do. She got dressed then went downstairs and rummaged through cupboards until she found a couple of candles.

Would she still be able to do this now that it mattered?

Callie took the candles out into the back garden, put them on a flat stone and set light to them with a thought.

She took a couple of deep breaths, then began to draw the flames upward to weave the net of lights that she hoped would protect the house. Of course, she had never tried to cast a net over anything this big... She hoped her parents weren't going to come home to a house that was missing one wall.

She had never concentrated so hard on anything in her life. She wove filament after shimmering filament together, felt, rather than saw the net grow larger.

Ready.

Callie cast the net of lights and watched it settle over the house, leaving all the walls intact. She gave a jump of triumph as she watched it flicker and disappear.

She'd done it. The house was protected. Nothing malevolent would be able to get past the net.

Perhaps she would have a shower after all. There was plenty of time. Josh wouldn't be round before ten.

After she'd showered and collected together the stuff she'd want on the beach she still had plenty of time, so she raided the fridge and made a huge picnic for them to take. She had just finished when the bell rang.

"You were right about the weather again," Josh said.

Callie looked smug. "What can I say? It's a gift. Do you want Dad's wetsuit again?"

"Yeah, please."

Callie fetched it and they packed the picnic.

"Back in a minute – I left my sunnies upstairs," she called to Josh, running up to get them.

Callie opened her bedroom door and let out a scream.

The room was littered with fragments of rock, some as big as a clenched fist. Water oozed through one wall and trickled into a grey-brown pool on the floor.

She heard footsteps running up the stairs behind her.

"Callie – what's wrong?" Josh looked over her shoulder into her devastated bedroom. "Jeez, Callie, what happened? It looks as though a bomb went off."

Callie had a hand over her mouth to keep herself from screaming again.

"Callie," Josh went on. "Should we call your parents? George and Rose?"

"No!" she said sharply. "Mum and Dad mustn't find out." She looked absolutely terrified.

"Why not? Your parents have to be told what's happened." He looked at the room again. "What *has* happened? I don't understand."

"It's my fault," Callie whispered almost inaudibly.

"*Your* fault? How can it be *your* fault?" Josh took a step into the room.

"No, Josh, don't go in! It might be dangerous." Callie slid down the wall into a heap in the doorway, put her face in her hands, and began to sob. "Please come out."

Josh picked his way over the rubble-strewn floor, crouched down and put an arm round Callie's shoulders.

"Callie, what is it? What's going on? How can this be your fault? You're not making sense."

"It *is* my fault. And I thought I'd protected the house, but I can't stop it getting in, because it's already here. It's *me*."

Josh had absolutely no idea what Callie meant.

"Come on, Callie. Get up. Let's go downstairs and get some stuff to clean this up. Whatever's happened here, it's not because of you."

She grabbed his wrist so tightly it hurt, and looked him in the eye.

"You're wrong. This is all because of me." She swallowed and blurted it out. "I'm a witch."

Half of him wanted to burst out laughing, but Callie was looking at him so fiercely that he didn't dare.

"What do you mean?" he asked lamely, playing for time.

"What do you think I mean?" she yelled at him. "I'm a witch. Somehow I'm making these things happen and I don't know how to stop them."

"A witch? Don't be daft, Callie. There's no such thing – not nowadays, anyway."

"Really? You don't think so?" Callie got to her feet, angry now instead of frightened, marched into her wrecked room and pulled a crumpled sheet of paper out of the waste bin.

"Watch," she said, and the paper burst into flames in the palm of her hand.

"What? How did you do that?" Mesmerised, Josh watched the blazing paper. "Callie, stop. You'll hurt yourself."

She closed her hand on the flames then opened her fingers to a trickle of grey ash and held up her hand, unburned, for him to see.

"I did it," she said slowly, "with witchcraft. I'm a witch. I'm a freak. I'm dangerous."

Josh took her hand in his and looked at it more closely, trying to make sense of what he had just seen.

He raised his head and looked at her white face.

"You're not a freak. You're not dangerous. You say you're a witch. Okay, maybe you *are* a witch – I don't pretend to understand that bit – but you're still Callie. You're Callie, and you're my friend. Tell me properly what's going on, so I can try to help."

She sagged into his arms with relief.

"You don't think I'm mad? You don't hate me? You're still my friend, even though I did this?"

Josh could feel her shaking in his arms. He had no idea what to do. He'd just have to make it up as he went along. He hugged her tighter.

"Why would I hate you?" he said over her bent head. "Of course I'm still your friend. And of course I don't think you're mad. I *know* you are. I've known that since the day I met you, so why should it make any difference now?"

"Oh, Josh, you don't know what a relief it is to have told you." She gave him an enormous hug, then stepped back, wiping her nose on her sleeve.

"Let's go downstairs," said Josh, "and you can tell me exactly what's going on, and then maybe we can work out what to do." As he spoke, his mind was replaying events from last summer: things that had seemed inexplicable at the time, but suddenly made perfect sense if Callie was a witch. It made such perfect sense that he couldn't believe he hadn't thought of it himself. Of course, he hadn't thought of it himself because it was impossible.

"Let's go into the garden," Callie said.

Sitting in the sun, she told Josh everything: Evie's broken arm, Rose's coven, her training and the escalating disturbances taking place around her.

"So now you know why it's my fault."

Josh didn't reply. The more he heard, the harder it became to disbelieve.

"Josh?"

He tried to reason his way through what he'd just seen and heard. "Why now? Why would this suddenly start *now*? You've known you're a witch for months, haven't you?"

Callie nodded.

"And you're getting better at controlling things?"

"Yes..."

"It doesn't make sense. Surely this would have happened when you had the power but you didn't know how to use it, if it was you causing it?"

"I... I don't know."

"Has anything happened anywhere except your house?"

"No. Just in the house."

"Well, if it was you, surely these things would happen wherever you were?"

Callie shrugged. "I haven't really been anywhere else since it started. Not for more than a couple of hours at a time."

Josh thought silently for a few minutes.

"Okay," he said. "Let's try to clear up your room, then you call your parents and ask if you can stay with me and Mum at the cottages tonight. If nothing happens while you're there, then it's your house, not you, making these things happen."

"But what if something does happen?"

"Then we'll deal with it. But you've got to tell Rose what's been happening."

Callie nodded. "I know. I thought I could sort it out myself, but..." She gave a rueful smile. "I'll go and see her on the way round to the cottages."

Something else had occurred to Josh. "Do your parents know that you're a witch? Wait – is your mum one too?"

Callie gave a mirthless laugh. "Dad doesn't know and Mum's mortified. She's not a witch and she's ashamed of me and of Rose. She definitely thinks I'm a freak."

Josh wanted to protest that she couldn't possibly, but something told him not to. Instead he stood up.

"Right. Let's sort your room out."

It took over an hour to get the bits of stone out and distribute them round the garden, mop up the puddle and clean the floor. At least water was no longer oozing from the wall. They moved a couple of posters and Callie's desk to hide the wet patch, then stood back to inspect the result of their efforts.

"Well, it looks okay to me," said Josh.

"You're not my mother," Callie pointed out unnecessarily. "She's like someone from *CSI*. It'll just take one bit of gravel and she'll work everything out somehow."

"They all do that, don't they?" said Josh, still scrutinising the room. "You get the place immaculate and they come home and take one look round and they're like, 'I see you had six friends round and ordered pepperoni pizza – sixteen inch – and drank nine cans of Irn-Bru and talked about films.' Honestly, mothers are a different species."

Callie was laughing now.

"With any luck she won't even come in here if I'm staying over at your place," she said, holding up crossed fingers.

"Has she texted back yet?"

"I left my phone downstairs. Let's go and check." Callie picked up her sunglasses, closed her bedroom door and led the way down to find that there was a text from Julia.

"Yes, it's fine," she said as she read it. "Now, what about the beach? I've had more than enough of this house, and there's a picnic that needs eating."

Lying on the hot sand, stuffed with food, surrounded by the noise of holidaymakers enjoying the sun, the situation seemed a little less daunting than it had in Callie's bedroom.

"So, tell me more about being a witch. Can you do lots of cool stuff? Do you have to meet with the rest of the coven at full moon?" Josh had been longing to ask, but he hadn't wanted to earlier in case it upset Callie again.

"And dance naked round a cauldron?" Callie interjected acidly.

Josh went scarlet and choked on his drink. "Don't do that," he wheezed in between coughs.

"Anyway, I can assure you there's no dancing, and no cauldron, and certainly no nakedness."

"Please, don't even make me think about that."

"And they don't worship the devil. Or have familiars," she went on, ignoring him.

"What about Luath? And Chutney Mary?"

"They're not familiars, you fool, they're pets."

"Well, what's the difference?"

Callie opened and closed her mouth. "Actually, I must admit I'm not sure."

"What about George?"

"I don't think he'd be very pleased to be described as a pet *or* a familiar."

Josh elbowed her in the ribs. "No, I mean what does he think about all this? I take it he does know?"

"Oh yes, he must know, but no one's ever actually told him, so he doesn't have to think anything about it. But I suppose the fact that he and Rose are still together speaks for itself."

When they tired of the beach, Josh and Callie dropped the borrowed wetsuits off. They'd gone into the house with some trepidation, but everything was just as they'd left it, and Chutney Mary accompanied them from room to room, purring cheerfully, tail high.

Callie collected her overnight stuff. She looked hard at the scruffy t-shirt and shorts she'd worn the night before. Nope. She rummaged through the drawer. There was a brand new set of proper PJs, still in the wrapper. She picked it up, then put it down again. What was she thinking? This was Josh, just Josh.

She was getting as bad as her mother.

She settled on a white I ♥ NY tee and shorts that weren't too grotty or too smart. Good.

"See you tomorrow, puss," Callie said as she shut the front door again.

+ + +

"Do you want me to come in?" said Josh as they reached The Smithy.

"No, thanks. I think I'd rather do this on my own," Callie replied. "I'll be along in a bit."

"Hello?" she called as she went in, but The Smithy was silent. There must be someone here, though; the front door hadn't been shut, let alone locked. She looked out of one of the back windows and saw George in the greenhouse, Luath lying in front of the open door like a draught excluder.

"Hello, George. Is Rose around?"

George put down his secateurs. "I'm afraid not. She went round to Miss Rutherford's a couple of hours ago with some flowers for her birthday – she's 87 – and found she'd had a fall. Rose has gone in the ambulance with her to hospital in Dundee, so I'm not sure when she'll be back."

"Oh..."

"I take it it's not something I can help with?"

"Not really," Callie said, perplexed. "It doesn't matter. I'll catch her tomorrow or something."

"That was quick," said Josh, answering the door.

Callie explained.

"I think you might be right about it being the house," she said, determined to be positive. "So tomorrow will do to tell her. It'll be fine."

Anna was working among a litter of papers in the sitting room.

"Some holiday," said Callie, with a smile.

"It's funny, it still feels like a holiday, even if I do some work, as long as I'm somewhere different," Anna replied. "Anyway, I'm not working every day. We had a lovely time in Falkland."

Behind her, Josh rolled his eyes.

"I'm just going to call your parents, Callie," Anna went on. "I'd better make sure they're okay with you and Josh staying in the same room. It's either that or one of you on the floor in here."

As Anna went to phone, Josh said, "I told her you'd been having nightmares and were scared to sleep on your own. Sorry; I thought it might persuade them to let us share."

"That's all right. It's a good idea. As long as you don't mind?"

Anna came back in. "She said yes. Thought someone else in the room might stop these bad dreams you've been having. I promised I'd keep an eye on you too."

"Please stop being embarrassing, Mum," Josh begged.

"I'm your mum – that's my job!" Anna said indignantly.

Later, when they'd had supper, Josh and Callie went for a walk. Not because they actually wanted a walk, but because Josh was desperate to see some of the things Callie could do with her nearly new-found powers.

"Honestly, though, there's not much I can show you. This isn't like magic on the television, you know," she protested. "It's not tricks and it's not Harry Potter."

"So you didn't have a 'Yer a wizard, Harry' moment?" Josh grinned.

"Eh, no. Not exactly. I had an 'Oh no, have I just killed someone?' moment and a table-bursting-into-flames moment."

"Whoa! What table? What happened?"

"When Rose and the others told me what I was, I accidentally set fire to the kitchen table in The Smithy."

Josh was wide-eyed. "Did you have to call the fire brigade? How come the house didn't burn down?"

"No fire brigade. Remember, I was in the same room as four proper witches. They put it out in a nanosecond. The wood wasn't even scorched. It wasn't normal fire, more like static, I think."

"Did you know before they told you?"

Callie wrinkled her nose. "I knew there was something... but I kept trying to convince myself it was all my imagination. I never thought I might be a witch until Rose said it."

"And you never knew that she was one?"

"No way! I thought she and Bessie and Barbara and Isobel were just four old dears who liked a gossip. I never noticed anything and I've known them all my life."

"So, what can you do?"

"Not much yet," said Callie, feeling suddenly self-conscious. "I can tell what the weather's going to do, but I can't control it."

"Rose and her mates can control the weather?"

"Well, a bit. They could push a shower out of the way, but not a rainstorm."

"Must come in handy."

"Yeah." Callie smiled.

"That fire thing you did – show me again."

Callie looked round. "Better go somewhere it won't be seen then."

"There's that ruined cottage down by the stream."

Five minutes later they were there, pushing aside swags of ivy to get through the remains of the doorway.

Callie picked up a stick and looked at it. Obediently, it burst into flame immediately, all along its length. She waved it like a conductor's baton.

Josh reached out to touch it.

"Careful!" Callie pulled it away from him. "You'll get burned."

"Why doesn't it burn you?" Josh asked, fascinated.

"Because I made the fire, and it knows I'm the boss. I kept getting burned when I was learning this, though; I'd be so pleased I'd managed to set light to something that I'd forget to control it."

She slid a hand along the length of the burning stick and the flames were gone.

"That's so cool," said Josh, shaking his head. "Show me something else."

"Tomorrow," Callie said. "I can't give away all my secrets at once." She was enjoying having something to show off about. It was an unfamiliar sensation.

"You might just be the most interesting person I've ever met. I'm definitely sticking around to see what else you can do."

Callie flushed with pleasure, turning away to hide it. "Better wait and see what happens tonight," she said, sobering. "Your mum might have forbidden you to see me again by tomorrow, or you might not want to."

8. SLEEPOVERS

Josh lay awake for a long time that night. Long after Callie's breathing told him that she was asleep in the other bed, he lay looking at the dim grey square of the window, his mind racing as he tried to sort out the day's events.

That Callie was a witch was actually crazily easy to accept, given her ancestry and her undeniable oddness. The stuff with the fire would have convinced him anyway, if he'd had any real doubts.

As to what was happening in her house... He was far less confident about that than he'd made himself sound. If something weird did happen during the night he hadn't a clue what he was going to do. Run away yelling, probably; if lumps of rock started falling out of the ceiling and the wall sprang a leak, definitely. Cool, logical explanations didn't seem quite so convincing, lying here in the dark.

He closed his eyes and tried to think of safe, dull, ordinary things that had nothing to do with witchcraft.

Something hit him in the face. With a sharp intake of breath he opened his eyes to find Callie, tousle-headed, sitting up in the other bed. It was broad daylight. Morning.

"Did you just throw something at me?"

"You were snoring. I had to stop you somehow. Anyway, it was just one of your socks."

"Yuk. I'm surprised you even wanted to touch it."

"*Wanted*? No. But it was the only thing I could reach without getting out of bed."

"Sleep okay?" Josh asked.

"Yeah. A perfectly ordinary night's sleep." A smile lit Callie's face. "Maybe you're right and this isn't my fault."

"So now all we have to do is work out what *is* going on and how to stop it. Simple. Breakfast first, though. I could murder a bacon roll."

"Ooh, yes please."

Anna was reading the local paper in the sitting room.

"Bacon roll, Mum?"

She looked up briefly. "No thanks."

Callie and Josh sat on the sofa and flicked absently through the TV channels as they ate.

"Well, here's an opportunity you don't get every day," said Anna, reading from the paper. "'Ever cuddled a lemur or stroked a skunk? Now's your chance! Fife Animal Park will be visiting St Andrews with some of our furry, feathery and scaly friends.'"

"Let's see," said Josh, cramming the last of his roll into his mouth. "Skunk stroking... Don't they make you smell terrible?"

Callie craned to see what Josh was reading. "Only if they're frightened, I think. Very gentle skunk stroking, maybe? A lemur, though... I've never seen one close up, and they look really cute on TV. Oh, it's today that they're in town!"

"Wanna go?"

"Yeah. Why not?"

"Okay, Mum?"

"Of course. I can even drive you in. I want to do some shopping." Anna reached over the back of the sofa. "Now give me back my paper. I've still to read about the Scout jumble sale." She paused. "What did you do to your wrist, Callie? That's a nasty bruise."

"Nothing," said Callie, self-consciously hiding the black mark on her wrist with her hand. "It's fine."

Anna went back to her paper without further comment. Josh looked curiously at Callie, but she pretended she hadn't noticed he was watching her, finished her roll and went to get dressed.

"What about going to tell Rose?" Josh asked when she came back.

"Let's go and see the animals first. It'll be a nice break from all this. I'll tell her when we get back."

When Anna dropped them at Kinburn Park in St Andrews, the animals hadn't arrived yet, so they strolled along Market Street to the sweet shop to stock up on trash, then walked slowly towards the park.

"Jelly snakes, mmnn..."

"You can't possibly think jelly snakes are better than white mice."

"Ten times better."

"Must be some weird witch thing."

Callie made a face at Josh. "I could turn you into a white mouse."

"No you couldn't."

"Maybe one day..."

"I can imagine Bessie turning someone into something."

Callie laughed. "I know what you mean, but she's all right, just a bit crazy. And, honestly, we can't turn people into anything."

Josh gave a theatrical sigh. "Another let down," he said morosely. "To change the subject," he went on, "we should be trying to work out what's happening at your house. We know now it isn't you making things happen, so why there and why now? When did it start?"

"It was two nights ago: the first day we went body boarding and then I went for my lesson with Rose and the coven. I heard hammering in my room that night, but no one else heard it.

"Then the next night." She shivered. "Same but worse, and a figure under the desk. It all stopped when my dad came into the room. The cat was going mental – that was what Dad heard, not the hammering. At least if Chutney Mary hears it, it's not just my imagination," she added thoughtfully.

"What sort of figure?" Josh asked, trying to sound matter of fact, though the hair was standing up on the back of his neck.

"I couldn't see it clearly. It was as if it was made out of darkness, darker than everything else around it.

It was human, though – well, human shape. I saw arms reaching up just before it disappeared... Can we stop talking about it for a bit?" Callie asked as they arrived back at the park. "Anyway, look; the animals are here."

They joined a queue of excited children and curious adults.

"Wow, look at that," Josh said as they got nearer. "It really is a skunk." He sniffed. "And I can't smell anything."

They shuffled forwards with the queue until they were close enough to listen to a talk about the animals. They stroked the skunk and a cockatoo, and fed grapes to a sleepy-looking black and white lemur. No cuddling, though: it held tightly to its keeper and didn't look as if it was ever going to let go.

"I wonder just how bad skunk smell really is?" mused Callie. "There was a tiny bit of me hoping I'd find out."

"Well, I just hope I'm not with you if you do," said Josh firmly.

A bit later, Callie got round to asking the question that had been on her mind for hours.

"Josh, can I ask you a favour?"

"Yeah, what?"

"Will you stay at my place tonight? I want to have one last try at dealing with this... whatever it is, without getting Rose involved. Getting a good night's sleep last night makes it all seem... a bit silly really. I think it's been a combination of witch power leaking out – sort of like static – and bad dreams, and everything getting out of proportion because I haven't been sleeping properly. It doesn't seem nearly as bad now looking back at what actually happened."

Josh looked doubtful. "You're sure it wouldn't just be easier to talk to Rose about it? You were all set to do it yesterday."

"I know. And yes, I'm sure it would be easier. But I must be feeling braver today or something. I really want to do this. Will you come?"

"How could I resist?" Josh said, with a certain amount of irony. "Remind me – have I ever told you you're crazy?"

"Of course." Callie was already texting as she spoke. "I should warn you – I've just said we'll cook tea. It'll stop Mum going overboard trying to entertain you. I'll try not to let her ask you too many questions."

Josh laughed. "It's okay. Honestly. So what are we cooking?"

"Not a clue."

They got back to Callie's house mid-afternoon, carrying prawns and dressed crabs. They picked strawberries and raspberries from the garden and made a summer pudding, then lay in the sun, having already checked that Callie's room was okay.

"So, what do we do tonight? Try to stay awake or try to sleep?" Josh asked, shading his eyes.

"Things have started when I've been asleep before,"

said Callie after a few seconds thought. "So I suppose if we actually *want* something to happen, we should try to sleep. I'm going to go up in a minute, though, and try to put a protective spell on the room."

"Can I watch?"

"Yes, but don't expect it to be exciting." She got to her feet, bent down to pick up a pinch of soil and put it in her pocket. "You'll see in a minute," she said, to forestall Josh's question.

Passing through the kitchen she collected a glass of water and a box of tea lights.

"What should I do?" asked Josh once they were in Callie's bedroom.

"Sit on the bed and don't say anything. I need to concentrate."

Callie put a candle in each corner of the room, one in the doorway and one on the windowsill, and lit them with a snap of her fingers, ignoring Josh's wild-eyed grin. Next, she picked up the glass of water and went from candle to candle, sprinkling a few drops onto the flames. The flames sizzled, but instead of being extinguished, they grew tall and translucent, more like molten glass than fire now. She went round once more, sprinkling a few grains of soil from her pocket onto each candle, and Josh saw the flames turn to the colour of dried blood.

Callie returned to the centre of the room, ignoring him completely now, her face serious.

"I call on the elements to protect this place and all those in it. I call on Air, I call on Earth, I call on Fire, I call on Water. Meld yourselves into a shield about this place. Let nothing wicked pass." As she spoke, the colour of the flames grew more and more intense, until they were like tongues of molten metal. "I draw you together with my power. Shield this place according to your natures. *Let it be so.*"

The flames grew so bright that Josh had to screw his eyes up, then they were gone, leaving no sign that the candles had ever been lit, not even a wisp of smoke.

Callie turned to look at him expectantly. "Well?"

"Looked pretty impressive to me, but what would I know?"

She sighed. "Well, it's all I can do just now." She looked at the clock. "I hope you're ready for the onslaught. The parents will be home soon."

"What do you miss about Edinburgh when you're here, Josh?" asked Julia, continuing her cross-examination.

Callie was mortified, but if Josh minded, he gave no sign of the fact.

"Nothing, really, when the weather's good. But if it rains I miss the indoor stuff you can do: bowling, cinemas, you know. And I miss the buses for getting around. I mean, I know you've got buses here, but at home they come much more often."

Callie was trapped between squirming embarrassment for Josh, and concern for her father, who had hardly said a word since he came in, and was now staring morosely at his crab and prawn salad, as though it was a particularly discouraging horoscope.

"You okay, Dad?" she asked, while Josh and Julia

were engrossed in twenty questions. David roused himself with a look of surprise.

"Yes. Fine. Just a bit down about life," he said with a sad smile.

Callie had never heard him say anything like that ever before. He never got depressed about anything. She felt a small, cold knot of anxiety develop in the pit of her stomach.

"What's wrong?"

"Nothing, just ignore me."

What could have happened? As if there wasn't enough to worry about already.

Callie had persuaded Julia that having Josh in the same room the night before had helped her sleep and that they should share here as well, although Julia had frowned when the question was raised.

"You said it was okay last night at the cottages," Callie reminded her.

"I thought it was just a one-off: some company to take your mind off these dreams. And it would have looked rude if I'd refused – as though I didn't trust Josh's mum. I'm not sure you ought to."

"Oh for goodness sake! We're not... there's nothing..." Callie could feel her face getting hot just thinking about the words. "I wouldn't even dare *ask* if... Look, we're just friends. I keep telling you that. Surely you can see?"

Julia gave her a long look. "Oh, all right. Josh's mum obviously thought everything went okay last night."

"Thanks, Mum," said Callie, with relief.

Callie finished shoving the pillow into its pillowcase and tossed it to Josh.

"Are you sure you don't mind a sleeping bag?"

"No. It's fine. Look, you've given me a mattress. That's practically luxury. I'm always sleeping on mates' floors at home."

They heard the sound of raised voices from downstairs. "What do you mean, it's my fault? You're the one who..." The rest of what David was saying was lost in the sound of a slamming door.

Josh tried to act as though he hadn't heard anything, but when he sneaked a glance at Callie's face it was obvious she knew he had.

"I don't know what's wrong with them. They don't usually argue, but recently... And there was definitely something wrong with Dad at teatime. Did you notice how quiet he was?"

"Yeah, but I didn't know if he was usually like that or not. Maybe it's their work. It must be pretty stressful being a doctor."

"I hope that's it. I wish they would tell me what's going on, though, instead of acting as if I haven't noticed."

"Have you actually tried asking them what's wrong?"

Callie shook her head. "I was hoping it would stop, but it just seems to be getting worse." She forced a smile. "Anyway, we've got other things to worry about just now. Bedtime?"

Josh glanced at Callie's alarm. Eleven forty. "Bedtime," he agreed. "Who knows, maybe it'll be like last night now you've put that spell on the room."

"Maybe." But Callie didn't sound convinced.

The sound of raised voices continued for another ten minutes, to be replaced at last by simmering silence.

Chutney Mary came scrabbling through the window, jumped onto the bed and settled down, purring.

"She seems happy enough," Josh said.

"Let's hope she stays like that."

They lay down to sleep.

Chutney Mary's hiss woke Callie instantly. She lay as still as a stone, breathing into the darkness, eyes wide, ears straining.

There was silence apart from the gentle *whuff whuff* of Josh's breath from the floor at the side of her bed. As far as she could tell, he was still asleep.

Callie waited. The cat was sitting up, staring into the opposite corner of the room, but there was nothing there that Callie could see. She licked her dry lips, wishing Josh was awake.

Five minutes passed and still nothing had happened. Callie began to relax a little. Maybe she'd imagined Chutney Mary hissing. Or maybe it was just coincidence. She looked at her clock. Ten past three.

"There's nothing there, cat," she whispered. Her voice sounded wrong. The sounds came out of her mouth and seemed to stop without travelling anywhere, not even as far as the cat, poised alert at her feet.

Chutney Mary suddenly gave another long hiss, jumped to her feet, and backed away from the foot of the bed, stiff-legged.

"Josh! Josh, wake up," Callie whispered urgently. "Wake up!"

Surely he wasn't going to sleep through whatever was about to happen?

Tap.

Tap. Tap.

"Josh, wake up!"

9. APPARITION

"Josh, wake up!"

He woke at last, with a gasp, and sat up. "What is it, Callie?"

Tap. Tap. Tap. Getting louder...

"Can you hear it?" she asked in a strangled whisper.

Josh nodded. "Yes."

The cat had backed herself all the way to the headboard and stood perfectly still and silent, tail bristling, the hair all along her spine sticking up.

Callie reached for her bedside lamp, but once again, instead of a reassuring flood of light there was only a wan flickering glow that shook the shadows but didn't banish them.

Hammering in the walls. All around them. Under them. Above them.

Josh flailed out of the sleeping bag, Callie stumbled out of bed and they stood, pressed together, listening as the crash of hammer and pick on stone grew louder.

"Do something, Callie," Josh gasped. "Some spell. Something."

He's right. I have to do something.

She searched her memory for a spell that would help, but what was left? She'd used two spells of protection and they'd made no difference at all. She felt the familiar prickling in her palms as she desperately tried to think of something. For once, she didn't try to push the power down. Could she focus it without using a spell at all, shield herself and Josh, blast whatever it was out of her room?

Callie felt power flowing into her, though she had no idea where it was coming from. She started to organise it, so she could use it against the unknown threat they faced, and began to build it into a shield.

And then a hand came up over the foot of the bed and gripped the mattress and a black figure began to pull itself out of the floor, and her mind went blank. All the power she'd been so carefully marshalling escaped her control and roared through the room like a whirlwind, smashing the window as it did so.

Josh and Callie clung together in horror as the dark figure emerged fully and crouched on the floor at the end of the bed. They could hear its rasping breath, but it seemed to cast its own pall of darkness and they could make out little apart from its human shape.

And still the noise battered at them, the noise of picks and hammers striking rock, over and over...

The figure stood up slowly, and at last Josh and Callie saw clearly what it was: a man, pushing dripping dark hair back from a battered face, patched red and black. Blood trickled from wounds all over his body; under a gaping flap of skin hanging from his chest, shattered ribs showed as white fragments. His left hand was missing, the arm ending in a bloody stump. A single, baleful eye stared at them.

"What are you? What do you want?" gasped Callie.

The figure opened its mouth to speak, but the sound seemed to come from the whole room.

We want what was taken from us. We want our lives. We want air. We want light. We were trapped for centuries. Now we want your lives.

Without warning, there was an explosion of sound and light and the air was full of fragments of stone and flying water.

Josh and Callie yelled in terror and crouched, hands over their heads, convinced they were about to die.

All the noise died away until there was nothing but their own gasping breaths in the darkness.

The door crashed open, the light went on and both Callie's parents burst in and stopped dead, mouths gaping.

Josh and Callie were huddled together against the far wall. The room was strewn with chunks of masonry and there was a gaping hole in the ceiling. A tiny functional part of Callie's mind realised that, looking up, she could sees stars: part of the roof was gone too.

"Oh my God. Callie, Josh, are you all right, are you hurt?" Julia stumbled towards them, closely followed by David. "What happened?"

David looked around. "It's the chimney. The chimney's come down. You could have been killed!"

Josh and Callie looked around them in silent bewilderment as David and Julia pulled them to their feet.

"Let's get out of here in case anything else goes."

As she was helped from the room, Callie stopped. "The cat! Where is she?"

"It's all right, love. She shot out as soon as we opened the bedroom door."

As they made their way downstairs, Callie felt her legs begin to quiver. They only carried her as far as the sofa before they gave way.

Josh was next to her, still silent, but she could see that his hands had begun to shake. They looked at each other, faces white with plaster dust as well as fear, hair clogged with grit and wood and paint, each thinking how awful the other looked.

"Your face is bleeding," said Callie, and reached out to touch Josh's cheek, her fingers coming away red.

"It's all right, Josh, it's nothing much, we'll get it cleaned up in a minute." Both Julia and David had switched automatically to doctor mode. "Here." David handed them each a bowl of hot water and a towel. "Wash that muck off your faces before it gets into your eyes."

Julia brought blankets through; both Callie and Josh were shivering with shock now.

"Right, Josh, let's see that cut." David peered at the wound as he cleaned it. "It should heal okay. I don't think it'll leave a scar." He put a couple of Steri-Strips on to close it. "Should be good as new in a few days. Keep these on and try not to get them wet. I'll check it in 48 hours." He stopped. "I sound like a doctor, don't I? Not your friend's dad. Sorry."

"That's all right," said Josh. It was the first time he'd spoken since the events upstairs. "It's quite reassuring."

"Right. You two stay there and take it easy. You've had quite some fright. Julia, let's go and have a proper look at the damage."

"Dad, no! It might be dangerous."

"Don't worry, we'll be careful."

Callie and Josh were left alone to contemplate what had just happened. *This is it,* thought Callie. *This is where Josh tells me he doesn't want anything to do with me any more. I don't really blame him.* She searched in vain for something to say. At her side, Josh was equally silent.

He's trying to think of a way to tell me he never wants to see me again. I should say something, make it easy for him. I don't know why I ever told him anyway. It's not as if there's anything someone like him could do to help. It's just made things more complicated.

She still couldn't think of anything to say, so they sat on in silence until Julia and David reappeared a few minutes later.

"There's nothing we can do until morning," said David. "Then we'll have to get a builder – or maybe a roofer – to look at the damage."

"Josh, I'll take you back to East Neuk Cottages in a few minutes. Do you want to phone your mum first?" asked Julia.

"Do I have to go? I mean, I will of course, if I'm in the way, but it doesn't seem worth waking Mum in the middle of the night when I'm okay."

Callie stared at him in astonishment. He'd just turned down a chance to escape. Why?

"You should go," she heard herself say.

"Do you want me to?" Josh looked puzzled.

"No, but after what happened..."

"You can stay if you want, Josh. Let us know one

way or another in the next ten minutes," said Julia, and followed David out of the room.

As soon as they were alone, Josh turned to Callie.

"What was that... thing... that came out of the floor? Did you see the state it was in?"

She shook her head. "I've got no idea. Could you hear it when it spoke?"

Josh nodded. "No air, no light, trapped for centuries... You know what this is about, don't you? That noise beforehand... I knew I'd heard it somewhere else, but I couldn't think where until just now."

"It's the tunnel under the castle," said Callie. "I should have worked it out before. I've been hearing the tunnellers. That's why all this started when it did."

"Callie, you have to tell Rose what's been happening. You can't possibly sort this out; even I can tell it's much too strong. Sorry."

She sighed. "You're right. I'll go and see her in the morning."

"Do you want me to come, or would you rather I didn't?"

"Come, if you're sure you don't want to bail on me."

"How often do you have to be told, you idiot? I'm not bailing on you."

Callie gave a smile of relief. "Mum," she shouted, "Josh is staying."

It was already growing light by the time anyone tried getting back to sleep. Julia and David eventually went back to bed, and Josh and Callie curled up in their blankets on the sofas. To everyone's surprise, they did sleep.

"Nervous exhaustion," said Julia, when they sat bleary-eyed over toast and coffee at breakfast time.

"Will your mum be up by now?" Julia asked.

Josh looked at the clock. Eight fifteen. "I expect so."

"I'll give you a lift round then, and explain what's happened."

"Builder's coming at nine thirty," said David as he came in. Both he and Julia had taken the day off work to deal with the crisis. "The insurance office is just on voicemail. I'll try them again at nine."

Anna opened the cottage door.

"Josh – what happened to your face?"

"It's been a long night," said Julia. "Can I come in and explain?"

When the explanations were over and Julia had gone, Anna sat looking at her grubby son.

"You could have been killed." She touched his cheek gently.

"Mum, I'm fine. Don't fuss." He got up. "I'm going to have a shower."

"Good idea. Your face isn't too bad but your hair looks as though you've just finished a shift in a coal mine."

If she only knew, he thought.

+++

At half past ten Josh and Callie met at the corner of the field by The Smithy.

"Did you have any trouble getting away?" Josh asked.

Callie shook her head. "No. They're engrossed with builders and roofers and insurers."

Josh started for the gate. "Just a minute. I want to talk to you before we go in," Callie said.

They both sat on the dusty verge.

"I haven't told you everything," she said. She pushed up her sleeve, so that Josh could see the dark patch on her wrist and the angry, inflamed skin that now surrounded it. "It appeared just after we went into the tunnel that day. It's been getting bigger and itchier ever since." She covered it again. "I've known all along it had something to do with things, but I didn't want to admit it to myself, never mind anyone else. I thought if I was the only one who knew, maybe it wouldn't be true." She grimaced. "I know how lame that sounds."

"Something else happened to you in there, didn't it? Not just claustrophobia or a panic attack?"

"When the lights went off, I heard voices," Callie admitted after a moment's silence. "Someone saying my name. Telling me to stay in there in the dark. Something touched me." She shivered at the memory. "There was something down there."

Josh's mouth was suddenly dry. "I know," he said. "I saw it, but I've only just realised. When you bolted, I thought I saw you crawling up the tunnel just ahead of me, and then you'd gone when the lights came back on. I thought it was you, but it wasn't. I think it was whatever you heard down there. Maybe we brought it out with us and into your house."

There was silence again as they went over in their heads what had happened that day.

"It all fits," Callie said slowly. "But why now? Why us? Think how many tourists must go down there every year."

"Ah, but how many witches go down?"

"Oh no... then it *is* my fault."

"Callie, that's not what I meant. You know it isn't. We need to find out more about the tunnels. What happened in there? You said there was a battle – maybe it's something to do with that. What have we brought out? What was that thing I saw? Look, it's time we told Rose everything. She'll know what to do, won't she?"

"I hope so."

They got up, walked through The Smithy garden and pushed the front door open.

"Rose?" called Callie.

An indistinct reply came from upstairs, then, "Just coming."

Through the window, they could see George with his back to them, busy in the greenhouse.

"Callie, Josh, hello," said Rose, coming down the stairs, and then, as she saw their faces, "What's happened? What's wrong?"

10. TRACES

Rose listened without interrupting to their hesitant, sometimes incoherent account of what had happened over the last few days, her lips compressed in a tight line.

Finally, Callie said, "I thought I could deal with this myself, but I was wrong. I'm sorry. I should have told you sooner."

Rose gathered her thoughts.

"First things first: no one was hurt when the chimney came down?"

"No."

"And what state is the house in now?"

"Mum and Dad are there with a builder and a roofer and the insurance people. There's a big hole in the roof where the chimney fell through. Hasn't Mum called you?"

Rose shook her head. "We're not really talking at the moment."

Callie looked stricken, but said nothing. Rose returned to the more immediate problem.

"I think Josh may be right about what's at the root of all this. It's certainly nothing that's coming directly from you. If it was, it would have happened before you started to learn to control your power. I don't think

116

anyone should be staying in that house overnight just now. Callie, you'll come here, won't you?"

Callie nodded.

"And you're all right at the cottage, Josh, aren't you?"

"Fine."

"I'll phone Julia and suggest she and David come here until the roof is fixed. Maybe if David answers the phone he'll accept my offer before Julia has a chance to refuse." She got to her feet. "Make us all some coffee while I do that, Callie."

The kettle had just boiled when Rose returned from phoning.

"Well?" Callie asked.

"I spoke to your father. He'll talk to your mother and call back." She made a face. "Oh well, I've done what I can for now." She sat down to drink her coffee. "The three of us need to go to the castle."

"You don't want me to go down there again, do you?" said Callie, alarmed.

"No, dear, don't worry." She glanced over at the washing-up bowl sitting expectantly beside the sink. "We need to talk to Bessie. I'll treat us all to lunch."

"Well, Rose, this *is* nice," said Bessie, settling herself in her seat and making sure she had a good view of the other diners just in case any of them did something interesting.

Josh stared, mesmerised, at her hat. It seemed to be knitted out of crimson string, and was decorated with three rather threadbare pheasant feathers. "It's my Thinking Cap," she said to Josh when she noticed him gawping at it. "A bit like Sherlock Holmes and his deerstalker. It compensates for electrical fluctuations in the brain."

Josh nodded, speechless, as Rose shook her head and muttered something none of them could quite hear.

"Callie, dear," Bessie went on, "you look a bit peaky. I hope you're not coming down with something?"

"I'm fine, Bessie. I just haven't been sleeping very well," Callie replied with stupendous understatement.

"That's why we wanted to talk to you, Bessie," Rose added.

"Well, I would usually recommend a wee nip of whisky, but you're a bit young for that."

Rose raised her eyes to heaven. "That's not going to solve this problem. Let's order, then we'll explain."

It took all the pasta and half the ice cream to explain the situation to Bessie.

"So now we need to find out what happened in those tunnels in the past, and who – or what – this figure could be." For once, there was no trace of Bessie's normal levity in her voice. "There have never been reports of people having uncanny experiences down there that I know of."

"I thought it might be because Callie's a witch, not a normal – sorry, I don't know how else to say it – person," said Josh.

Bessie gave him a narrow-eyed look. Josh hoped she wasn't putting a spell on him. He prepared himself to find he had grown whiskers, or something worse.

"No," she said firmly. "It can't be that. I've been down there more times than I can count." She saw Josh and Callie exchange glances. "When I was younger and more... athletically built, I mean. I'm not exactly the shape for shimmying through wee holes like a ferret now. But witches aren't *that* rare. There must be tourists who have power in there every year."

So witches aren't that rare? Josh filed that one away for further consideration.

"No. This is something more specific, and we need to find out what." Bessie ate her last spoonful of ice cream and pushed away the bowl. "Right. I think we should get back to the castle and have a poke around behind the scenes."

"But not down the tunnel?" Callie asked, just to be sure.

"Definitely not."

"Hello, Margaret, that's me back from lunch," said Bessie brightly to the woman behind the desk at the castle. "I've just brought my friends along for a wee look at some books in the office."

Margaret looked doubtful.

"That'll be fine, won't it, Margaret?" said Bessie, looking at her intently.

"Oh yes," said Margaret, smiling. "That'll be fine."

Did she just? No – surely not... Josh remembered the way the tourists had left the castle shop so suddenly when he was last here, but there was no chance to linger as Bessie marched them past the desk and through a door, shutting it firmly behind them.

She switched on the light. "Welcome to my kingdom," she said. "Now, where to start?" She stared at a wall of books, tapping one foot as she thought.

Rose had already selected a volume, and she sat down at a wooden table to look through it, once she'd moved a plate of shortbread and several mugs out of the way.

Josh spotted a computer at the other side of the room.

"Can I use the internet?" he asked.

"Be my guest," said Bessie absently as Callie drifted over to the computer with him.

An hour and a half passed in almost complete silence as Josh and Callie trawled the internet and Rose and Bessie searched book after book. It had been easy enough to get at the bare bones of the story, but beyond that they had all drawn a blank.

"There's not much on the internet about the castle and hardly a mention of the tunnels," said Josh. "I can't believe there's not more. There's got to be *something* about who dug them and what happened down there."

Bessie got up to switch the kettle on. "Let's pull together what we've all found," she said. "Whatever went on happened in 1546 during a siege. That much is certain at any rate."

"And it was religion at the bottom of everything," added Rose. "Cardinal Beaton, who was Catholic and controlled the castle, was imprisoning Protestants there. Not just imprisoning them, either. Some were burned alive."

"George Wishart," said Callie. "I remember that from history at school."

"It says here," said Josh, reading from the screen, "that friends of the murdered Protestants tricked their way into the castle and murdered Beaton in revenge."

"And then the ruling Catholics besieged the castle with the Protestants stuck inside," added Callie.

Bessie handed out cups of tea and made space again on the table for the shortbread. "I know this bit," she said. "The siege went on for five months, and the besiegers got fed up, so they started to dig a tunnel in from outside. But the people *inside* found out what was happening, so they dug their own tunnels to try and find the one coming in. Eventually they broke through into it and there was some sort of battle. Now, what else have we got?"

Silence.

Rose spoke up. "The Protestants were defeated in 1547, but that's nothing to do with the tunnels. I couldn't find anything more." She looked at the others.

Bessie shook her head.

Callie said, "We couldn't find anything on the net either."

"There must be a way to find out who was down there and what happened to them?" said Josh, exasperated by their lack of progress.

"Would Margaret or any of the others know more, Bessie?" asked Rose.

Bessie shook her head. "They'll only know what's in the books here." She drummed her fingers on the table as she stared into space.

Rose put her tea down and addressed herself to Bessie again. "Are you thinking what I'm thinking?"

"We need to do a reading?"

Rose nodded.

Josh looked at Callie, hoping for an explanation, but she just shrugged.

"What's a reading?" he asked Rose.

"When anything happens, it leaves a trace in the surroundings."

"You mean like fingerprints, DNA, that sort of stuff?"

"No," said Bessie. "You've been watching too many crime programmes. It's more like a recording."

"And the more dramatic the event, the more powerful people's emotions at the time, the stronger the recording," Rose went on. "Now, somewhere like a beach, or a wood, the trace wouldn't last long, because the physical surroundings change – the tide carries things in and out, plants grow and die. But it would last longer in a house, because it would get into the walls, into the stone. And in a tunnel that's hardly changed since it was dug..."

"It should still be there even now?" Callie guessed.

"Exactly," said Rose. "So in theory, we just need someone to go down there to... access the recording."

"Someone who doesn't have any power of their own that might interfere with it," Bessie added.

Three pairs of eyes swivelled to look at Josh.

"Ah," he said. "That's me, isn't it?"

"But surely that's dangerous for Josh?" Callie protested.

"No. Nothing will happen to him. It might be a bit... unsettling... but he'll come out again absolutely fine," Rose said quickly.

"It'll be just like being a television set," said Bessie bafflingly. "We can watch, but whatever the TV shows doesn't affect the TV, whether it's war, or illness, or weather, or one of those awful reality things. The TV isn't harmed."

Josh hadn't particularly enjoyed his first experience of the tunnel, and he didn't relish the idea of going down again now, especially on his own, but if it would give them answers...

"You don't have to be down there alone," said Rose, as if she'd read his thoughts. "You can wait until other people go down. Just not us."

That wasn't so bad.

"And you're sure I won't bring anything back out with me?"

"Absolutely," said Rose firmly.

"All right. I'll go down."

"Good lad," said Bessie. "Right. Sit down here and we'll get you ready."

"Get me ready? What do you mean?"

"Oh, it's nothing. Just a wee laying on of hands. Unless you think you could do the job more effectively as a rat?"

"Stop it, Bessie!" said Rose sharply. "Pay no attention to her, Josh."

Josh sat down rather reluctantly.

"Just relax. You can close your eyes if you want. Bessie and I are just going to tune ourselves in to your mind, so we'll know what's happening when you're down the tunnel."

"Does that mean you'll be able to read my thoughts?" he asked, alarmed.

"I knew you were going to say that," said Bessie, staring owlishly at him. "Och, only kidding! No, of course not. We're not going to be rummaging round in your mind as though we're at a jumble sale."

"What about me? Can I tune in as well?" asked Callie.

"You don't have the skills for this yet, I'm afraid."

Rose and Bessie each put a hand on either side of Josh's head, while he sat there feeling like a complete idiot. After a few seconds they moved away.

"Is that it?" He'd been expecting something more, though he wasn't sure what. Chanting, or a tingling sensation or something. His head exploding.

"That's it. Now we can tune in. It's just up to you to decide when to go down."

"The sooner I get it over with, the better. I'll go when I see someone else going in. But what do I do once I'm in there?"

"All you need to do is put your hand flat somewhere on the stone and stand still for a couple of minutes," said Bessie.

"Will I feel anything?"

Bessie glanced at Rose. "Maybe nothing at all. Or you might glimpse things, hear things happening. Just remember, it's only a recording."

"Where in the tunnel should I do it?"

"That's a good point," said Rose. "Because, of course, it's actually *two* tunnels." She considered for a moment. "I think you should try at the foot of the stairs at the far end first, then come back up the ladder and try again in the narrow part."

"Okay."

"I suppose I'd better let Margaret back into the office now," Bessie said.

As they went out, Callie spoke quietly to Josh.

"Are you sure you're okay with this?"

"There doesn't seem to be another way. We've got to find out what happened down there. I'll be all right as long as the lights stay on this time." He tried to sound more cheerful than he felt, but he wasn't quite sure he'd pulled it off.

They loitered on the sunlit lawn at the centre of the castle ruins, waiting for someone to start down the steps to the tunnel. It was only a few minutes before three American students paused to look at the information board and decided to go in.

"Here goes," said Josh, and he headed after them.

Physically, the tunnel was just as Josh had remembered it – the sloping floor and the awkward bent-kneed shuffle that was necessary to avoid braining yourself – but full of American accents and laughter, any threat it had held a few minutes ago melted away.

Piece of cake.

He waited his turn to descend the ladder and

cautiously stood up straight again. The Americans were taking photos. Lots of photos. Josh edged past them with a smile and leaned against the wall at the foot of the steps as though he was looking at the light drizzling down through the manhole cover. He put one palm flat on the wall, spread his fingers and waited for something to happen.

He could still see the Americans, but either they had stopped talking, or he couldn't hear them any more. Instead, there were fleeting snatches of conversation buzzing through the air around him.

How much further?

About twenty feet or so.

And how much longer?

That conversation faded out to be replaced by another.

Hush! Be quiet and listen.

What are we listening for?

Someone else digging.

I hear it!

And faintly now, Josh too felt the sound of hammer and pick on stone. He kept listening, but there was nothing else he could understand, just buzzes and whines and half-heard words. It was like listening to a badly tuned radio.

He gave it five minutes and took his hand away. That should certainly be long enough: Rose and Bessie had said a couple of minutes would do.

The Americans had gone back up the ladder and were taking more photos in the narrow tunnel. As Josh reached the upper level he saw them making their way out, but he didn't mind. The lights were on, he could see daylight from the entrance, and transmitting the recording – if that really was what he'd been doing – had been no problem at all.

He decided he may as well be comfortable, so he sat down at the side of the tunnel and put his hands flat on the stone floor...

Perhaps hell will be like this.

I wipe sweat off my filthy face, try to ease my spine. The tunnel is far too low to stand up.

Something hits me in the back and I sprawl on the muddy floor. The commander's boot.

"Get up, boy! There's no time for idling. Get back to work."

I pull myself to my knees and grip the handle of the pickaxe.

"Get on with it, boy, or you'll feel my boot again."

"Aye, sir." It's not what I want to say. I swing the pickaxe.

I am living in a nightmare.

11. DUNCAN'S STORY

I am living in a nightmare.

The three of us work in silence, for all the good that does. The hammers and picks make more noise than our voices ever could.

I am sweating again, partly from effort, but mostly from fear. The tunnel has had three false starts, but now the commanders are convinced we are digging in the right direction. That means, of course, that at some point we will break through into the besiegers' tunnel. I am afraid to think further than that.

I should have stayed safe in Pitmillie.

I came here to work in the kitchens, then the Protestant rebels tricked their way in and murdered the Cardinal, and suddenly I'm down in the black dark, digging, stuck in the middle of a siege. I shouldn't be here. I should be with Elspeth.

Every few minutes we stop and listen, but there is nothing but the drip of water and our own harsh breathing. The flames of the stinking tallow candles flicker with each breath.

Please God, don't let them go out and drown us in darkness.

Without warning, earth and small stones begin to shower down from the roof.

"Get back!"

We scrabble across the uneven floor like spiders. Is this the cave-in that we dread all the time?

The trickle of earth slows, stops.

"Right, it's safe. Get back to work." The commander's voice again.

Safe? How does he know it's safe? Safe for him, at the mouth of the tunnel. They're all the same, afraid to soil their hands, for all their talk of fighting, making kitchen lads like us do the dangerous work.

"I said, get back to work." A heavy hand hits me round the head and a wave of anger snaps through me, leaving my skin tingling.

"Why don't you take a turn?" The words burst out of me before I can stop them. "Are you feared your hands will get dirty? Or are you just feared?"

The commander swings a fist, but he must be off-balance, because his feet shoot out from under him and he goes down like a felled tree. His head hits the rock wall with a cracking sound as he falls.

The others stop digging, stare at him, then at me.

"What have you done, Duncan Corphat?"

"I never touched him. You know that. I lost my temper and shouted, but I never laid a hand on him."

It is true and yet it is a lie, for I know I did this. The tingling in my skin... it comes when Satan's power works in me. I have tried, often and often, to pray it out of me, but it will not leave.

I am surely damned.

I think of Elspeth again, fleetingly, something bright among all my dark thoughts. But that too turns to anger. I should be with her. It's near her time. I should be there, not rooting in the dark here like a mole.

My blood runs thick with anger and I feel the treacherous tingling again. I try to ignore it, take up the pickaxe once more and go back to work. After a moment, the others follow.

Hammer on rock. Drip of water. Half an hour has gone by, and still the commander doesn't move.

Have I killed him?

I am too afraid to go and see. The metallic taste of fear is in my mouth. I am in hell, doomed to swing this pickaxe over and over again until the world ends.

"Stop!" the single word is a desperate whisper. A finger points at the rock wall.

A pinprick of light. Coming through *the wall. The other tunnel!*

God have mercy.

They must have heard us. They must be waiting for us.

We creep back, silently. It's soldiers they need down here, not kitchen boys. We get perhaps a dozen feet and then the wall detonates in front of us.

I hear screaming, but I do not know if it comes from my throat. The treacherous power comes sweeping through me and there is no chance, no time to control it.

Satan is coming for me.

The power explodes out of me like thunder, and...
"Josh?"..."*Josh?*"..."JOSH!"

Someone slapped his face and he gasped a breath and focussed his eyes. Callie stared at him, wide-eyed with fear.

"Josh? Can you hear me?"

He looked round in confusion.

I'm Josh. That's right. I'm Josh, not Duncan.

"What happened?" He pulled himself to his feet, grabbed the handrail for support and, without waiting for an answer, started hauling himself towards the entrance to the tunnel, Callie on his heels.

He emerged into sunlight and fell to his knees ,gasping for breath, unable to comprehend what had just happened to him. Callie was beside him, speaking to him, but he couldn't take in what she was saying.

He heard the sound of other voices and lifted his head to see Rose and Bessie hurrying towards him.

"I'm all right," he managed to say, and with Callie's help got to his feet, pushing his hair back from his sweaty forehead.

"Josh, dear, are you all right? We had no idea you would be affected like that," said Rose, "or we never would have asked you to do it."

"I'm fine," he said brusquely, walking away from the gaping tunnel entrance. He ploughed determinedly all the way across to the seaward side of the castle, Callie mute at his side, leaned over a railing and was sick down the cliff.

After a few seconds he straightened up and turned away from the rail, wiping his mouth. Rose and Bessie had sat down on a bench some distance away.

"You look terrible," Callie said. "What happened?"

"I don't know." He looked at her properly. "You look pretty awful yourself."

"You were in there for ages," she went on. "What were you doing?"

"It was only a few minutes."

"Josh, it was nearly twenty minutes. That was why I came down." She shivered. "Rose and Bessie knew something was wrong, but they didn't know what. We kept thinking you'd come out, but you didn't, so I had to come down and you were just sitting there, staring into space."

"They said nothing would happen to me." Josh looked over at Rose and Bessie, who looked anxiously back at him. "They lied to me to make me go down there."

"No, Josh, honestly. You should have seen them. They had no idea what was going on. They were really worried. They wouldn't have asked you to go down if they'd thought anything could happen to you."

"Do they know what I saw?"

"I think so. But I don't. Will you tell me?"

"I don't want to have to go over it more than once." He took a deep breath. "I'll go and talk to them as well."

He walked across to Rose and Bessie and sat down at the end of the bench, as far from them as possible. Callie sat next to him.

"Feeling better?" Bessie rummaged in her handbag and handed Josh a bottle of water. He took it without answering and swallowed several mouthfuls before he spoke.

"Did you know what would happen to me?"

Rose's shock was apparent. "Heavens, no. We would *never* have sent you in there if we'd expected anything like that to happen."

"What *did* happen to me?"

"I don't know," said Rose.

"Perhaps it's because you've been in the tunnels before, and then had contact with whatever it is we're dealing with at Callie's," suggested Bessie.

"Maybe that's somehow sensitised you to what's down there," added Rose, nodding.

"But nothing happened the first time I did it – in the big tunnel. I heard a few voices, but that was all."

"It was the emotion that did it – it was so much stronger at this end of the tunnel. That's why it affected you so much more."

Rose leaned across and put a hand on Josh's shoulder.

"If it's any comfort at all, we've learned a huge amount from what you went through."

"Will someone *please* explain to me what Josh saw, what we've found out?" Callie almost shouted.

"Yes, of course Callie. But not here, I think. Can we go to your house, Bessie?"

"I think we'd better."

Twenty minutes later they were sitting in Bessie's garden. Callie looked as though she might burst if someone didn't tell her very soon exactly what was going on.

"You start, Rose," Bessie said.

"All right. Bessie, Josh, stop me if I miss anything out or you think I've got something wrong.

"The people who dug the tunnel *out* from the castle – that's the narrow bit – weren't soldiers, just castle servants," Rose continued. "They were young lads from the surrounding villages, who hadn't much interest in the vendetta that had trapped them inside the castle. They weren't soldiers, they weren't miners, but they were suddenly expected to become both. They were angry, but most of all, they were frightened.

"At least one of them was from Pitmillie: a boy called Duncan Corphat, a bit older than you are now."

"Duncan Corphat? Why is that name familiar?" Josh asked.

"Janet Corphat," replied Callie. "We found out about her last summer, remember? She was one of Agnes Blair's witch friends."

"That's right. This was about a hundred and fifty years before they were alive, mind you," said Bessie. "Josh, can you remember what Duncan was feeling?"

Josh nodded. "Yeah. It's still very clear." He closed his eyes for a few seconds. "He was really, really frightened. And he was angry he was being made to dig. But..." he cast about for the right words, "it was as if he was afraid of *himself* more than anything. I think he worried that he was possessed. He kept talking – no, thinking, I suppose – about Satan's power flowing through him. He'd tried praying, but it didn't help. He'd feel a tingling and the power would break loose."

Callie drew a sharp breath. "Did you say tingling?"

"That's right."

Callie looked from Josh to Rose and Bessie. "Now it makes sense. Duncan Corphat was a witch. Somehow, it's him doing all these things, isn't it?"

"We think so," said Rose.

"But he didn't know what he was," said Bessie. "So

134

he'd had no help from anyone to deal with the power. It just broke out when he got angry, so he thought it was a sign of evil."

"He thought he'd hurt the commander," said Josh excitedly. "Maybe killed him."

Rose nodded. "We saw that."

"Okay," said Callie. "So Duncan Corphat was an untrained witch, and that's what all this power is that's ricocheting round my house, but that still doesn't explain why it was *me* that it latched on to. You said there'll have been witches down there every year. Why not one of them? Why me?"

"Hang on, hang on," Josh interjected. "You keep saying Duncan was a witch. Surely you mean a wizard? Witches are always women, aren't they?"

Bessie tutted. "Indeed they are not. Wizards don't do anything useful. They're just daft men who like to dress up and wave sticks around. Any excuse for a party. Witches can be men or women, and *they're* the ones who have real power. There have been a good few male witches round here over the years."

"Though none since John Fordyce died," interjected Rose. "I think that line must have died out with him."

"Now, Callie, back to your question – and it's a good one," Bessie continued. "The answer's in the poor lad's name and where he's from."

"Duncan Corphat from Pitmillie," said Rose. "No one moved around much in those days. Lots of people were born, married and died without ever leaving their village. He must have been quite adventurous to have got as far as St Andrews."

"Do you think he was an ancestor of Janet Corphat?" Callie asked.

"Yes I do," Rose said. "And Agnes Blair," she added. "And you. I think perhaps it was from him that all the Pitmillie witches down the years inherited their powers."

There was silence in the room.

"But wasn't Duncan killed in the tunnel?" asked Josh. "Surely that explosion..." He stopped as something suddenly occurred to him. "Wait a minute; there were *two* explosions. Was the first caused by the besiegers and the second one because of him? Was it Duncan's power that brought the roof down?"

Rose nodded. "I think it was, from what we saw just now. And yes, I'm sure Duncan must have died when the tunnel collapsed, or his memories wouldn't end so abruptly. Poor lad," she said sadly.

"But he can't be my ancestor if he died without having children, and you said he was just a young lad," Callie protested.

Rose ignored her for the moment and spoke to Josh.

"Can you remember what Duncan was thinking when they went back to digging after the commander's accident?"

"He was furious that he was stuck in the castle. He wanted to go home to Pitmillie."

"Why?" Rose coaxed.

"There was a girl... Elspeth. He wanted to be with her. He said her time was near. What does that mean? Was she dying?"

"It means she was pregnant. This Elspeth was expecting Duncan's child and her time to have the baby was near. They might have been married. People sometimes got married very young back then. You couldn't count on living to be old."

"Poor Duncan," said Callie quietly. "He thought he was possessed by the Devil, he died under the ground trapped like a rat, and he never got to see his child. That's awful. No wonder he brought so much anger out with him.

"It all fits together: the reason he attached himself to me is not just because I'm a witch; it's because I'm a witch who's descended from him."

"And who hasn't fully taken control of her power yet," added Rose.

"But wouldn't there have been others who went down between fifteen whatever and now?" Josh wasn't quite convinced.

"The tunnel was blocked off for centuries," Bessie replied. "It was only rediscovered a hundred-odd years ago. How many half-trained witches from Pitmillie who're descended from Duncan Corphat do you think have been down there?"

"Probably just the one," he had to admit.

12. CONFRONTATIONS

Callie kept rubbing at the black mark on her wrist as Rose drove back to Pitmillie. It was definitely bigger than it had been yesterday.

There wasn't much conversation in the car, as the three of them tried to absorb what they'd learned in St Andrews.

Josh felt slightly disconnected, part of him still embroiled in Duncan's memories. How long would it take for them to fade, he wondered.

Now that she had an explanation for what was going on and why, Callie felt more optimistic about the situation, in spite of the dark blot on her arm. She felt sorry for poor Duncan Corphat. She wanted him out of her house, but she also wanted to help him. All these years with part of his mind – spirit – soul – whatever it was – trapped and helpless in the dark. At least she could tell him that his child must have survived.

Rose dropped Josh at the cottages, and she and Callie got out at The Smithy.

"Ask your dad if they want to stay here tonight," Rose reminded her. "And George and I will see you later."

"All right."

As she walked home, Callie could see a tarpaulin had been fixed over the hole in the roof. Apart from that, the house looked normal, from the outside at least.

She let herself in and went into the sitting room to find her father slumped in an armchair. He didn't even acknowledge her.

"Dad? How are things?"

He looked at her as though he wasn't sure what she meant. After a moment, he spoke.

"It's all falling apart. The house is just the start of it. Everything's coming apart: house, marriage, work. There's no point trying to stop it."

"What? Dad, what's wrong? What are you talking about?"

"I'm tired, Callie. I don't want to talk just now."

Callie's heart was thumping. She was baffled and very worried. She'd never seen her father like this. "Did you decide if you're going to stay with Rose until the house is sorted out?" she asked, desperate for some sort of normal response.

"No," he said. "There's no point trying to run away."

"I'm going to talk to Mum," Callie said.

Her mother was in the kitchen, a half-drunk bottle of wine and an empty glass on the table in front of her.

"Where have you been?" she snapped as soon as Callie put her nose round the door. "You've been with that boy again, haven't you?"

"Mum, you know I have. I told you this morning. You

said it was fine. You wanted me out of the way when all the workmen were here."

"I don't remember saying that." Julia obviously didn't believe her.

"Mum, what's wrong with Dad? He's just sitting there. He says everything's falling apart. I'm worried about him."

"Worried about *him*?" There was acid in Julia's voice. "This is all his fault."

"No, it's not! How can it be his fault that the chimney came down?" Callie leapt to her father's defence.

"Do you really think that's all that's wrong with this family? A chimney? A hole in the roof? You're more stupid than I thought."

Callie felt sick. She didn't understand. She wanted to run away. "What's wrong with you?" she yelled. "What aren't you telling me?"

Julia poured a glass of wine. "There's nothing to tell you. You know it all, don't you? That old woman's filled your brain up till there's no room left for your own parents. You love her more than you love me."

"That's not true!" Callie shouted. "You know it's not."

The familiar, ominous tingling spread out from the back of her neck all the way to her fingertips. Without warning, the bottle and glass shattered.

The silence that followed was broken by the sound of wine dripping from the table.

"Hah!" scoffed Julia. "I was right. You still can't cope with it."

Callie fled before she did something worse, running

out of the house and down the road all the way to the beach until she ran out of breath and dropped to the sand among the dunes.

She tried to keep her mind a blank, to let it fill up with the sounds of the sea and the gulls, the smell of seaweed, the sight of small clouds drifting across the sky. Anything was better than thinking about what had just happened.

After a while, she sat up. Now that she was out of the house she could think more clearly and her parents' behaviour seemed even more bizarre.

Now that she was out of the house...

"Idiot," she chided herself.

How could it have taken her so long to realise? What was going on with her parents was part of this... haunting, or whatever it was. She had to get either her parents or Duncan Corphat out of the house.

With the idea clear in her head now, a lot of recent odd exchanges between her parents were explained, as were some of her own crazier thoughts.

Callie got to her feet. It was time to do something.

While she walked away from the beach, Callie planned her next moves. First she had to get her parents out of the house, preferably to stay at Rose and George's. Once they were safely out of the way, she was going to talk to Duncan Corphat. She'd explain to him as best she could what had happened, tell him he had descendents, and that she was one of them. She'd show him what he'd done to the house and tell him to leave. He wasn't evil, he was just trapped, maybe hadn't realised he was dead. Once he knew, surely he would go? He had no reason to want to harm anyone here.

Simple.

"I'm not going there. Don't be ridiculous."

In a wild change of mood Julia had begun to spring clean the kitchen, turning out cupboards to scrub them. "I don't know what plan you and she have thought up, but forget it. This is my home. She can't have it."

Callie's plan already seemed less straightforward than it had fifteen minutes ago. Her mother sounded completely intransigent, so she turned her attention to her father.

He was sitting where she'd left him, but he'd been busy too. He was surrounded by shiny scraps and held a pair of scissors. Callie realised with a jolt that he was cutting up the photos from the family albums one by one.

"What are you doing?" she gasped. "Stop it. Stop it!" She pulled the scissors from his unresisting grasp and chucked them through the window into the garden. He'd have to go outside if he wanted to get them back.

She took his arm. "Come on, Dad. Let's go to Rose's. You'll feel better there, I promise."

David shook her hand off. "I'm not leaving. If I leave now, Julia will never let me back in." He looked at her through narrowed eyes. "Are you part of this too?"

Callie gave a groan. She was never going to get them out of the house by herself. She went into the bathroom for some privacy and tried to call Rose, but her phone had no signal for some reason, and when she tried the landline, instead of a dial tone there was just a series of clicks and whistles.

How dare Duncan Corphat do this to her? She would show him power; she would make him regret his interference in her life.

Callie ran upstairs and threw open her bedroom door, and a gust of cold, damp air hit her in the face. She paused on the threshold, taking in the scene before her. The light in the room was tinted a sickly green by the tarpaulin over the roof. The floor was several centimetres deep in water. Why hadn't it seeped through to the rooms below? It lapped up to the doorway and stopped dead, as though held back by some invisible barrier. Rocks lay everywhere, from pieces of gravel to a head-sized boulder that had smashed her bed. Water oozed from the walls in a reddish trickle.

In one corner of the room lay a void of utter darkness, waiting for her.

Callie stepped into the remains of her room and closed the door, so angry that there was no space left inside her for fear.

"Duncan Corphat," she said, "show yourself."

The blackness wavered like a flame caught in a draught, and from it, Duncan Corphat began to emerge.

He had probably been a good-looking boy once. Callie could see he had black hair, and the eye that he still had was blue. His left hand was gone, his chest smashed, his body mangled by the explosion and the cave-in that had followed it.

143

He stared at her, oblivious of his physical state.

"Are you Duncan Corphat?"

Yes. The answer seemed to come from the whole room, not just from the broken figure in front of her.

"Get out of my house. Leave my family alone. We've done nothing to you. I don't know why you're doing this, but you must stop. You're dead. You shouldn't be here."

We had done nothing to those that killed us. But that didn't matter to them, the room breathed.

"It was you who killed yourself. You didn't understand the power you had. You still don't."

The dreadful figure's eye blazed with anger. "Get away, girl, while you still can. You do not know what you speak of." This time the voice came more directly from him.

"Oh, but I do. I understand the power you felt in you. I'm your descendant. You had a child, and you passed on your power. I have it too. Look." Callie scooped a handful of the icy water from the floor and set it aflame.

"Witch!" His voice was like falling rocks. How was it possible for her parents to hear nothing?

"Yes," she said. "Like you. That was the power in you, but you let it destroy you."

"I am no witch!" the figure screamed. She could feel the power crackling between them like static now.

"Get out of my house!"

No. The voice came from all around her as the water that seeped from the walls turned, before her eyes, into flame, and the whole room was ablaze around her.

She yelled the words that should kill fire, but while it shrank back from her a little it did not go out.

Water. How to conjure water? What were the words? What had she been thinking, to face this alone? It was as though Callie had suddenly been slapped awake, aware of the awful danger she was in.

The flames blazed brighter again. Callie thrust her arms above her head and desperately stammered the words of the water spell, heard the flames sizzle in the downpour she had somehow called, saw them crumple and die.

Run girl. Run while you can.

Breathless, Callie pulled the door open, sprang through and slammed it shut. No sound came from the room behind her. She sealed the door with a spell so that her parents couldn't wander in by accident.

Rose. She needed Rose. Now. She pulled her phone from her pocket, then remembered it was useless. She stumbled into the bathroom, half-filled the basin with water and breathed on it.

"Rose, help me. He's too strong for me. Come quickly."

13. THE SPELL OF COMPULSION

Callie waited anxiously in the road until Rose appeared and started talking as soon as she got out of the car.

"What were you thinking to challenge him like that, Callie? You weren't prepared."

"You're right about that. And I don't think it's just him. He talked about '*We*'. '*We* were killed.' I think he's brought out the memories of the others who died with him, but he's much the strongest."

"We'll think about that later," Rose said, checking in her handbag for a number of things. "We have to get David and Julia out of here first."

"I told you: I tried. They won't leave."

"They'll leave for me," said Rose grimly. "Now, Callie, I'm going to have to put a spell of compulsion on them. I'll deal with Julia first – she'll put up the most resistance. Ignore anything she says; it isn't really her talking. Your job is to stop her from interfering with what I have to do to set the spell. Do you understand? You'll have to physically keep her away from me if necessary. If we're lucky, I'll be able to build the spell before she realises I'm in the house."

As quietly as she could, Callie opened the front

door again and they crept in. As they went past the sitting room she glimpsed her father still rooted to the armchair, his back to the door, destroying more photographs. Deprived of the scissors, he had simply begun to tear them up.

They ducked quickly into the dining room and pushed the door almost shut. Rose put her bag on the far end of the table and began to bring things out. Three candles. A bunch of herbs. Callie recognised feverfew and sage and goosegrass, but not the others. A salt cellar.

"I need a hair from each of them."

Callie pictured herself creeping up on her parents and trying to yank out hair without them noticing.

"Not like that!" Rose's whisper was uncharacteristically sharp. "Hairbrush. Comb. Clothes."

"I'll have to go upstairs."

"Go."

Callie tiptoed upstairs and into her parents' bedroom. It was a shambles. It looked as though someone had emptied every drawer and cupboard onto the floor. A half-packed suitcase lay open on the bed.

She picked her way round the debris and found Julia's hairbrush, plenty of dark hairs caught in the bristles, but she couldn't see her father's comb anywhere, despite poking around under the heaps of discarded clothing.

Just as she was starting to think she might have to pull a hair out of his head, she saw a woollen hat he sometimes wore in the winter. When she looked closely, she could see a couple of short, brown hairs caught in the wool.

Clutching the hairbrush and the hat as if they were treasure, she crept back to the dining room.

Rose looked up from her preparations and saw what Callie was carrying.

"Good girl," she said.

The candles were lit now, their flames twined into a little basket in which the herbs lay, not burning, but floating as though they rested on water.

"What else?"

"Salt," said Rose, sprinkling it over the herbs. "Then the hairs, then the words of the spell. It'll only take a couple of minutes now." She peered at the hat and pulled a hair loose, dropped it into the basket.

Intent on their preparations, Rose and Callie failed to notice the door opening until a shriek of anger made them jump.

"Get out of here you old crone, and take *her* with you!" Julia stood in the doorway, hair awry, a can of polish and a duster in one hand.

"Good evening, Julia," said Rose calmly. "George and I were hoping you would stay with us while the house is put to rights."

"I'd sooner sleep on the streets," Julia spat back. "Take your filthy magic and your little... familiar... and get out of my house."

She advanced into the room and Callie moved to block her path.

"Really, dear, there's no need to be unpleasant about this. Why don't you polish something and let me get on here?" Rose went on placidly.

Callie glanced round to see her pulling some hairs

from the brush and adding them to the basket. Rose waved a finger and the basket closed round its contents like a glass bubble, and floated, a clear globe, above the table.

"Callie, dear, I need to concentrate for the next couple of minutes. Perhaps you would talk to your mother?"

Callie nodded.

"I don't want to talk to you," said Julia with a brittle laugh. "I've been talking to you for years and it's made no difference. Do you know how hard it is to love you?" Callie felt as though she'd been punched in the stomach. "Always different. Always awkward. Why couldn't you be *normal* like everyone else's children? Why did *I* have to give birth to a freak?"

Dimly, Callie heard Rose's voice speaking the words of the spell behind her. Her mother was right, of course: she was a freak. She'd tried to convince herself it wasn't true, but of course it was.

"You're right," she heard herself say, though she hardly recognised her own voice. "I am a freak. What do you want me to do?"

"What do *I* want? When have you ever taken notice of that?" Julia leaned forward so their faces were only a few centimetres apart. "I. Don't. Care," she said in a poisonous whisper. "Go off with that deadbeat boy. Go and live in filth with the other witch. Go and die. I don't care." Julia took a step back and smiled at her.

She couldn't speak. She couldn't move. She couldn't breathe.

"Callie."

"Callie!" Rose's voice. Callie took a breath. "It's not her. It's not your mother talking, it's Duncan. It's part of the haunting. She doesn't mean any of it. Now stand aside. The spell's ready."

A hand on her shoulder moved her out of the way, and Rose faced her daughter, the clear globe and its contents floating between them.

"Get that thing away from me!" Julia batted at the globe, but her hand passed straight through as if it was an illusion.

"I'm sorry, my dear, but we have to get you out of here."

"No! I'll never let you have my house," screamed Julia, and spat in Rose's face.

Rose wiped her face on her sleeve and pointed a finger at Julia.

"I compel you," she said steadily. "You will do what I ask."

"No I won't!" Julia launched herself at Rose just as Rose clapped her hands with the globe between them. It disappeared into a faint yellow haze which enveloped Julia.

Julia stopped dead.

"That's better," said Rose. "Now, Julia, go and fetch what you need for a few days at The Smithy, then get into the car and wait for me. You and David are coming to stay for a while."

Without another word, Julia turned and left the room. Rose came forward and put an arm round Callie's shoulders.

"That was terrible, I know, but your mother didn't mean any of it. It's the effect of this house, of what Duncan Corphat is doing. You do know that, don't you?"

Callie didn't trust herself to speak. She nodded, but she didn't really believe what Rose was telling her. Since she found out she was a witch, she'd been afraid this was exactly the way her mother thought of her.

"You should go outside. Being in here isn't doing you any good either. I won't have any problems with your father now the spell's built."

"Okay."

She walked to the front door with Rose, the globe, which had rematerialised from somewhere, floating about Rose's shoulder like an eccentric balloon.

"Off you go," said Rose, and went into the sitting room.

Callie walked outside and sat on the wall, shaken to the core by the confrontation with her mother.

Rose is right, she told herself. *This is all part of the haunting.* But she couldn't rid herself of the fear that Duncan Corphat's influence had unlocked what her mother really thought, deep down.

Ten minutes later, Rose emerged from the house with Callie's parents, each of whom carried an overnight bag. They looked slightly distracted, but otherwise acted normally as they got into Rose's car, Julia smiling at Callie as though nothing had happened.

No one spoke during the short drive to The Smithy, but when they got there Rose said to David and Julia, "You've had an awful time. Why don't you go upstairs and unpack, then lie down for a rest before supper? I'll call you when it's time to come down."

"All right, Mother," said Julia.

"Thank you, Rose," said David.

George passed them on the stairs as he came down to the kitchen.

"I thought you might have been longer," he said. "So I haven't put the lasagne in the oven."

"That's all right," said Rose, moving to do just that. "Callie, do you want a rest?"

Callie shook her head. "My brain's in too much of a whirl. Can I put the TV on and find some rubbish to take my mind off things?"

"Of course."

"The cat's already on the sofa waiting for you," added George.

Callie felt a pang of guilt. She hadn't given Chutney Mary a thought all day.

"Did you go and fetch her?"

"No. She turned up of her own accord, just after lunchtime. Clever cat, that one."

The cat gave a chirrup when she saw her mistress coming into the room, and the moment Callie sat down Chutney Mary was on her lap, purring and milk treading as though they hadn't seen each other for days, not hours. Callie began to relax, just a little.

There followed one of the strangest meals Callie had ever had. Her parents had been called and had obediently appeared in the kitchen to take their places at the table. Rose and George acted as if everything was perfectly normal, keeping up a gentle flow of inconsequential conversation as they all ate. Julia and David took part in

152

it to the extent that they answered questions or spoke about a topic if Rose or George brought it up, but they never initiated any of the talk. Callie herself didn't say much. The day had been endless, and she wanted nothing more than an unbroken night's sleep.

But what about Duncan Corphat?

As she helped Rose clear up after the meal, she asked that question, dreading the answer.

"We're not going to do anything tonight. Everyone's exhausted; that's no state to face him in. Tomorrow we'll decide what to do next." Callie sagged with relief. "Now off you go to bed before you fall asleep under the table like the dog. You're perfectly safe here, and so are your parents. I should send them off to bed too." Rose glanced into the sitting room, where Julia and David sat placidly drinking coffee. "I don't suppose they've had much sleep either."

Callie slept through the night as though she'd been anaesthetised and woke ravenously hungry.

While she was shovelling in toast and peanut butter, her parents appeared in the kitchen.

"Morning," said George.

They replied with a general "Good morning," to everyone and sat down.

Rose put more toast on the table. "I expect you're both still tired," she said. "I expect you'd be quite happy just pottering round the house and garden today."

"Oh yes," said Julia.

"Sounds just right," added David.

"George will be around if you want anything. Callie and I have things to do."

"That's fine," said Julia with a smile.

"Come along, Callie. Let's get started."

Callie crammed the last half-slice of toast into her mouth and followed Rose out of the room. When she had managed to swallow, she asked, "What are we doing?"

"Consulting Bessie first of all," said Rose, leading her into the garden and lifting the lid of the water butt. "We'll get her to meet us at your house and then... we'll see."

Callie and Rose were just about to go out when the doorbell rang.

"Morning," said Josh. "Just thought I'd drop in and see what the plan is for getting rid of Duncan."

"There isn't a plan yet," admitted Callie, and launched into an account of what had happened since she'd last seen him.

"That's horrible," he said as she finished. "Are you all right? And your parents?"

"Everyone's fine," said Rose. "Callie and I are just off to meet Bessie and see what we can do."

"Will you come?" asked Callie. "I mean, you don't have to, but I'd feel much better with you there."

"Of course I'll come."

They walked from The Smithy this time, and got there at the same moment as Bessie arrived by car from St Andrews.

"Well, dear, open the door and let's see just how bad things are," she said to Callie without preamble.

They stopped just inside the front door and listened for a few seconds, then moved forwards to the foot of the stairs.

"Let's stop here for a wee minute," Bessie said, taking something out of her pocket. She bent to put four little cubes at the corners of an imaginary square on the floor.

"Wardstones," said Rose approvingly. "That's a good idea."

"What are wardstones?" asked Josh. The cubes looked a bit like dice or sugar lumps.

"Bones with protection worked into them," said Bessie. "As long as we stay within the square that they bound, we're safe from any manifestations."

"It acts a bit like a shark cage," Rose added.

"Bone," repeated Josh. "Human bone?" he asked hesitantly.

"But of course," replied Bessie with an incredulous look. "What else would it be?"

"For goodness sake behave yourself, Bessie," Rose scolded. "Of course it's not human bone, Josh, it's..."

"Deer, dear." Bessie couldn't resist, despite Rose's death-ray stare.

"Callie, let me see your wrist again," Rose said.

Callie stuck her arm out. "It's still getting bigger," she said gloomily.

Rose and Bessie considered the dark mark and both nodded in agreement.

"Right. You two wait outside while we go upstairs," Rose instructed them.

"No! I'm not leaving," Callie insisted.

Josh would have been more than happy to wait

outside, but one glance at Callie told him she wasn't going to find that acceptable.

"Neither am I," he said, trying to sound as if he meant it.

"In that case, you *must* stay within the ward square," said Rose.

"We mean it," added Bessie. "We can't be distracted worrying about you two if we're to have any chance of dealing with whatever it is in your room."

"All right." Callie sounded reluctant, but Josh was delighted.

"Ready, Bessie?"

"Ready, Rose."

Under Callie and Josh's anxious gazes, the two witches set off up the stairs. At the top they paused to listen at the bedroom door for a minute or so, before cautiously pushing it open.

This time, the water wasn't trapped by the invisible barrier. As the door opened it flowed out and cascaded off the landing and down the stairs like an indoor river. Within seconds all the downstairs floors were awash except for an island of dry carpet bounded by the wardstones.

"Crazy," muttered Josh.

Callie's eyes were fixed on Rose and Bessie. From where she stood she could see a little way into her room. The two witches had stopped just beyond the doorway. The air around them shimmered with protective spells. Heart thumping, Callie waited.

Rose and Bessie gaped at the room. Despite Callie's description, it was still a shocking sight. To their sensitive noses, the air was acrid with power, like the smell of lightning. For three or four minutes they did nothing, as the water rushed past their feet, trying to construct in their minds the flow and pattern of the power that had caused all this.

In the corner, the cloud of darkness brooded, waiting for them to turn their attention to it.

"What are they doing?" whispered Josh.

"Trying to work out what's been happening, I think."

"Then what?"

"I wish I knew."

Rose and Bessie studied the cloud.

"That, I take it, is whatever remains of Duncan Corphat?" asked Bessie.

"And the others who were working with him, according to what Callie said."

"Ah, what fun: a multiple entity. When did we last deal with one of those, Rose?"

"We never have, Bessie."

"That's what I thought." Bessie rolled her sleeves up. "Shall we begin?"

Rose nodded.

"Duncan Corphat, we call you forth."

The cloud swirled gently, like smoke in a draught, but no figure emerged from it.

Bessie added her voice, and they tried once more to summon Duncan Corphat.

"He's not exactly keen to come out for a chat," observed Bessie.

"I was afraid this would happen when I saw the mark on Callie's wrist," said Rose, ignoring Bessie's attempt at humour.

"You think he's linked himself to her?" Bessie looked at Rose, no levity in her voice now.

"That's exactly what I think."

"Callie," whispered Josh. It was the first time either of them had spoken for several minutes. "I can hear him. I can hear him in my head."

"What do you mean?" Callie glanced away from her grandmother to see Josh, white faced, with his hands to his head as though he was in pain.

"Josh, what's wrong? What's happening?"

"He's in my head," Josh gasped. "Duncan Corphat's in my head."

14. GRIMOIRES

"Rose!" yelled Callie. "There's something wrong with Josh." She took him by the shoulders and shook him.

"Josh, what's happening?"

"I can feel him. He's so angry. Get Rose and Bessie out of the room," said Josh with difficulty.

Callie glanced up the stairs. "They're already coming."

"Take him outside, Callie," Rose called.

Callie hustled Josh out of the front door and sat him down on the wall, where he took several deep breaths before taking his hands cautiously away from his head.

"Is he still there?"

"No. He's gone."

"What happened?" asked Rose, sitting down beside him.

"When you opened the door to Callie's room, he was suddenly there in my head, shouting curses."

"But that shouldn't be able to happen," said Bessie. She peered at the wardstones in her hand. "There's nothing wrong with these. Nothing should be able to get past them."

"Perhaps nothing did," said Rose thoughtfully.

"What do you mean?" asked Callie.

"If the wardstones were working properly, nothing

would get past them. That means whatever it was came from *inside* the ward square," Bessie expanded.

"But the only things inside it were me and Josh," protested Callie.

Bessie raised her eyebrows, but said nothing.

"Let's get away from the house a bit before we talk," suggested Rose, so they started towards the beach.

"We had long enough in your room to find out something crucial about Duncan Corphat's haunting," Rose began, trying to think of a way to cushion the blow she was about to deliver.

"Yes?" said Callie eagerly.

"I'm afraid it means that Bessie and I can't get him out."

"Will you need Barbara and Isobel as well? Can I help?"

"That's the thing. It's not a case of more people. It's the *right* people that matter. The right *person*."

Callie stopped walking, the pit of her stomach dropping away with the awful certainty of what was coming.

"That's me, isn't it?"

"I'm afraid it is."

"But why?"

"The thing we're calling Duncan Corphat is a distillation of all the fear and anger that were in that tunnel. It – he – made some sort of connection with you when you were down there. The black mark on your wrist is the physical evidence of that. Your power and his are connected now, and I fear you're the only one who can get him out of your house."

Callie was horrified. "But I told you what happened when I tried yesterday."

"Yes, I know. But you weren't prepared then, and neither were we. We'll find a way for you to do this, Callie."

"What about me?" said Josh. "Why could I hear him when no one else could?"

"You're tuned in to the right frequency, since you went down the tunnel for us," Rose replied. "You're sensitive enough to pick him up here, now that he's getting more powerful. It won't happen as long as you stay out of the house."

Josh nodded. He just hoped they were right this time.

"It's not just getting him out that we have to think about, though," cautioned Rose. "It's what we do with him afterwards. We can't simply shove him – it – them – back in the tunnels under the castle. The fight he would put up would put the whole of the surrounding area, never mind us, in far too much danger."

"So what do we do with him?" asked Callie.

"I have no idea."

Callie floated on her back, her ears full of water, trying not to move so much as a finger. The chlorine in the water made her eyes sting, but she kept them open, staring at the wood panels of the roof. She caught sight of a shape from the corner of her eye and Josh surfaced and shook the water out of his hair like a dog.

When they had arrived back at The Smithy after their

161

fruitless attempt to evict Duncan, they had found the house empty and a message from George saying that he had taken Julia and David down to Fife Ness to do a spot of birdwatching.

"If I had any doubts my spell had worked, that would lay them to rest," observed Rose dryly. "It'll be the first time Julia's watched a bird in her life."

Josh had suggested Callie come back to East Neuk Cottages with him, and Rose had encouraged her to go.

"It'll take your mind off things for a while. Off you go. Try to relax. There's nothing you can do here anyway."

At the cottages, they had found the car missing and a note from Anna to say she'd gone to Dundee, which happily meant they didn't have to invent an alternative version of the morning's events.

"Watch this," said Callie as Josh blinked the water out of his eyes.

She kept absolutely still and pulled herself through the water using her mind alone. Josh grinned in amazement as she swept past him as though powered by an invisible motor.

"C'mon, give me a shot," he pleaded.

"You can't do that!"

"I know that, but maybe you can do it to me."

Callie stood up. "I hadn't thought of that. Let's see. Lie on your back and keep as still as you can."

Josh did as she said. Callie held her hands above him as if she was warming them over an invisible fire. After a few seconds, she moved them to the right, and to Josh's – and Callie's – surprise, Josh moved along like a puppet on a string.

She gave a delighted laugh. "Wow. I never knew I could do stuff like this."

She moved her hands the other way, more forcefully this time, and Josh went sailing off to the left, chuckling as he went.

Callie snapped her hands to the right again, and Josh whizzed past her, laughing like a maniac, at such a speed that he left a wake, and she had to stop him with another gesture before he crashed into the pool wall.

"Now that was fun. I thought you said there was nothing good about being a witch?" Josh said, wiping his face. "Maybe we could just book Duncan into one of the cottages for a few hundred years, and you could teach him how to do that. I bet he's never been in a swimming pool. Might improve his outlook a bit. It would be better than roaming around as a ghost or getting shoved into some grave."

For a second, Callie felt as though she was on the verge of remembering something important, but it was gone before she could grasp it. With a sigh, she headed for the ladder at the edge of the pool.

"Why are you getting out?"

"I want to be at The Smithy when Mum and Dad get back from Fife Ness, just in case the spell's worn off or something and Rose needs help."

"Okay."

Rose heard a car stop outside, and the sound of voices and happy barking: George and the others back from their constitutional. She'd tried to reassure Callie that she wouldn't be needed, but Callie's face had just taken on that stubborn look she knew too well.

"Hello Mother, hello Callie," said Julia happily as she came in.

"Had a nice time, dear?"

"Lovely, thank you, Mother. We saw some birds."

"Goodness me, that must have been interesting."

"Yes, it was."

Rose was beginning to think she preferred Julia like this. An unworthy thought, but there you were.

"Would you and David like to cook today?" she said, ignoring a twinge of conscience that knew this wasn't what spells of compulsion were for.

"Ooh yes. I like cooking," said Julia enthusiastically. "I'll go and see what you've got. Come on, David."

Rose looked at Callie. "Satisfied?"

"I suppose so. Sorry. Where did you take them, George?"

"Along the beach from the golf course as far as Constantine's Cave then back across to Longman's Grave and along Dane's Dyke."

Callie stared at him.

"What? Did I do something wrong?"

"No. You're a genius. That was it. That was what I almost remembered before."

"Should I have any idea what you're talking about?"

"No. Definitely not."

Rose eyed her granddaughter curiously. "Keep an eye on Nigella Lawson and Jamie Oliver in the kitchen for me, would you, George?" she said.

When they were alone, Rose turned to Callie.

"What is it?"

"Longman's Grave. George's story," Callie said excitedly. "He was told the Longman sometimes takes the unquiet dead down into the underworld to protect our world. Maybe we can persuade him to take Duncan. What do you think?"

A slow smile spread over Rose's face. "I think I'd better phone Bessie."

"It's Rose. I know what we can do with Duncan."

"That's a relief, because I've got no idea," said Bessie.

"It was Callie's idea, clever girl. I should have thought of it myself, mind. So should you."

"Please put me out of my misery, you irritating woman."

"Dane's Dyke. Longman's Grave."

There was silence on the line for a few seconds.

"You think we can raise the Longman?" For once, Bessie's voice betrayed doubt.

"I think we have to try."

"I'll go and dig up the grimoire and come over at six."

"I'll have mine by then too."

Just before she put the phone down, Rose heard Bessie mutter, "We must be off our heads."

She checked that George and the chefs were still occupied in the kitchen, went out to the garden and collected a spade from the shed.

There was a white-barked birch tree in one corner.

Rose counted five paces along the wall from it, two out, and struck the spade into the soil.

Just as well George hasn't planted anything really precious here in the seventeen years since I put my grimoire away.

About a foot down, the spade hit something. Rose knelt down and brushed soil from the surface of a stone slab, about fifteen centimetres square, with an iron ring at its centre. She got a couple of fingers through the ring and heaved. Seventeen years was a long time, and at first nothing happened. She picked up the spade again and gave the stone a good whack, hoping to loosen it. This time when she pulled, the slab shifted, and she was able to drag it out of the hole.

Beneath it lay the rest of a small stone box, and snug inside was a bundle wrapped in black plastic. Rose put it in her pocket, replaced the stone lid and roughly filled in the hole again.

Back in the house she could feel the grimoire in her pocket, heavier than its size suggested it should be. Heat leaked from it, but she didn't dare put it down anywhere in case someone else picked it up and opened it.

She hoped Bessie remembered where she'd buried hers.

Bessie arrived half an hour later, looking flustered.

"It's not happy about having been buried," she said, as they stood round George's work bench in the garage.

"Neither is Duncan Corphat," said Rose briskly. "They should get on like a house on fire."

"There was a tree root cuddling it. I nearly took the end off my foot with a hatchet trying to get at it."

Bessie looked at Rose properly. "Seriously, Rose, how long do you think it is since anyone tried to raise the Longman?"

"I've heard stories of it being done, but I've never heard of anyone who's actually done it."

"Me neither," said Bessie gloomily. "Certainly not in our lifetime."

"Do you know how to raise him?" Josh asked.

"There are various things we can try," said Rose, a bit evasively. "Callie, you should see this. It will be yours one day." She took the packet containing the grimoire from her pocket.

"Should *he* see this, Rose?" Bessie asked sharply, gesturing at Josh.

Rose sighed. "Josh is so deeply tangled in this that I hardly think it matters if he does. Who would he tell, anyway? He'd just make himself a laughing stock."

"I wouldn't tell anyone about any of this," Josh protested, offended.

Bessie nodded, apparently satisfied, and bent to take something out of her handbag. She set a package wrapped in a flowery tea towel on the table beside Rose's.

Rose raised an eyebrow. "Does it not object to that?" She gestured at the tea towel.

"It needs reminding that I'm the boss. That seemed an easy way to do it." Bessie looked at the tea-towel-wrapped object sternly.

Josh wondered what on earth could be inside. A familiar, maybe?

"What are they?" asked Callie as Rose and Bessie began to unwrap the parcels.

"Grimoires."

When Callie looked blank, Rose added, "Spell books. They're passed down from witch to witch. Mine will pass to you when I die."

"It doesn't look as if you use them very often," Josh observed, watching the unwrapping.

"The spells in a grimoire aren't the sort of spells you use every day," said Bessie. "We haven't used ours in seventeen years. They've been buried since then. It's safer for them and safer for us. You don't want to keep a grimoire where you can pick it up and leaf through it on a whim."

She laid a small, thin book bound in faded red leather on the table. Rose put a similar book with a black binding next to it.

Callie's eyes were wide. "Why haven't you told me about this before? How old is it? What sort of spells are in there? Can I look?" She reached out to pick up Rose's grimoire and was shocked when Rose slapped her hand away.

"Don't touch!" she said sharply, then, more gently, "These are dangerous things, Callie. Why do you think we're not doing this in the house? You're not ready for them yet, but you will be, one day."

"Sorry." She still couldn't take her eyes off the little book.

"Ready, Bessie?" Rose asked.

"Yes," said Bessie, getting to her feet. "Best stand back a bit, you two. You can never be quite sure how these things will react."

The way they spoke about the books made Josh wonder if he ought to pick up one of the hammers from George's toolbox, just in case.

They pointed at the grimoires and their covers slowly opened. Josh saw pages that were yellow with age, covered in handwriting that was indecipherable from where he stood.

The pages turned themselves slowly, one by one, Rose and Bessie peering closely at them. Callie and Josh watched in silence.

Occasionally one of the books would pause somewhere while Rose or Bessie considered a spell more closely before the pages began to flicker by again.

After about ten minutes, Rose suddenly said, "Bessie, I think this might do the trick."

Bessie transferred her attention to Rose's grimoire, and her own snapped shut, almost as though it had taken offence.

"I doubt we'll find anything better," she said after a couple of minutes. "Shall we?"

Rose nodded, and the two witches each put a hand on the open pages of the grimoire.

The book twisted and bucked at their touch as if it was trying to escape. Josh and Callie took a step back from the table. They could see how hard Rose and Bessie were having to push down to stop the book shaking itself loose from their hands. A wisp of smoke drifted up from the binding.

"Don't you dare!" said Rose sharply, and suddenly the book was still, as though the fight had gone out of it. "That's better," she said, tucking a strand of hair that had come loose behind her ear with her spare hand.

As Josh and Callie watched, the ink seemed to lift away from the paper and coil round their fingers like the tendrils of a plant. It sank into their skin and disappeared, leaving the open pages blank. When Rose and Bessie lifted their hands away the grimoire closed softly with a sound like a weary sigh.

"I didn't think we'd have to fight the spell out of the pages of that one," said Bessie. "Mine was always more temperamental than yours."

"Even mine has its little ways."

"You're talking about those books as if they're alive," Josh said, trying to inject a moment of reality.

Rose and Bessie stared at him.

"Your point is?" Bessie said in a combative tone.

"Well, they're... they're just books."

"Of course they're alive," said Rose, as though it should be perfectly obvious. "They're *grimoires*. They wouldn't work if they weren't alive."

Josh opened and shut his mouth. Really, faced with a statement like that, there was nothing he could say. He turned to Callie, who raised her eyebrows and shrugged. Clearly she had no more idea about all this than he had.

"So," she said to the room in general, "now what?"

"Now we have to get you ready to winkle Duncan Corphat out of that house, and ourselves ready to raise the Longman from his grave," replied Rose. "So you'll be having a crash course in advanced witchcraft for the rest of the day, and tonight we make our move."

"Does it have to be at night?" asked Josh. "Isn't it safer in daylight?"

"We can't raise the Longman in the middle of the day," said Rose. "We can't have someone blundering across him in the middle of a family walk."

"No," agreed Bessie. "We need to do this when as few people as possible are around."

"Er... there's one thing we haven't mentioned yet," said Rose, carefully meeting no one's eyes. "Duncan needs to be transported from the house to Dane's Dyke."

"Can't you drive us?"

"That's not what I mean exactly, but Bessie and I will have to be down at the dyke before you get there."

"George, then? Or I could..."

"Callie, just listen, would you?" Rose interrupted in exasperation. "I'm not talking about cars. Duncan Corphat needs to be secured... inside a *person*."

"And that's me," said Callie.

"No, that's *not* you. You'll be busy imprisoning him in the other person."

There was a short, awkward silence.

"You mean me, don't you?" said Josh slowly.

15. THE WITCHES' PLAN

Rose looked uncomfortable.

"If I was sure that either Bessie or I could raise the Longman on our own, then of course it would be one of us," she said. "David and Julia are no good and George... George would do it, but I've spent nearly forty years trying to keep him out of things, whereas you're already involved in this." She looked at him steadily. "I know I've no right to ask this of you."

"What if Callie puts Duncan into me, but you can't raise the Longman, or he won't take him? Am I Duncan for ever? Half Duncan for ever?"

"Absolutely not," said Bessie crisply. "If necessary, we'll simply let him loose at Dane's Dyke, and everyone will just have to avoid the area. We'll know to, anyway, and it'll soon get a reputation as a place to keep away from."

"That doesn't sound very good."

"It's not, but there's nothing else we'd be able to do."

Josh tried to think, but it was almost impossible. Rose and Bessie looked at him silently, waiting for a reply. Out of their line of vision, Callie was giving him a death stare. She shook her head, mouthed, *Don't do it*.

He looked back at her and knew he had to. "All right," he said, hoping he didn't sound as scared as he felt.

"Thank you, Josh," said Rose, relief clear on her face. "You should go home now; see your mother, have a rest, have something to eat. Will you say you're coming back here to spend the night or will you have to sneak out of the cottages later?"

"I'm not sure. I'll see what Mum says, then text Callie."

"That's fine."

"Come on," said Callie. "I'll see you out."

When they were alone in the front garden she rounded on him furiously.

"I don't want you to do this. You shouldn't have let Rose talk you into it."

"She didn't. I decided."

"You can't do this. I'll have no idea what I'm doing. What if something goes wrong? What if Duncan *does* become part of you for ever?"

"You heard what Bessie said."

"Yes. But she doesn't know what she's talking about either. They've never tried anything like this before. Just because they're witches doesn't mean they know what they're doing. This could all go wrong."

"Look," said Josh slowly, "if this was happening the other way round – if I was the witch and you were me – would you walk away now? Would you really leave me to deal with this on my own?"

"I don't suppose so," Callie replied reluctantly.

"Well, I'm not going to either. We can only do this together. There's a link between us now; you know that." He took a breath. "I'll see you later," he said, and left her standing there.

When Callie went back inside, Rose looked at her quizzically, but said nothing. Instead, she picked up the grimoire, safely sealed inside its waterproof wrappings again.

"Come on. You should know where this is kept, just in case you ever need to dig it up," Rose said to Callie. "After that, Bessie and I are going to force-feed you as much advanced magic as you can hold."

She cast a look at Bessie's tweed skirt and polished shoes.

"You'd better go home and change into clothes that are a bit more suitable for grave opening."

"I'm sure I've got the perfect hat somewhere."

Callie was sweating. She, Rose and Bessie were closeted in Rose's little sitting room with the windows and door firmly shut and seven candles burning in front of them. Bessie was now wearing a pair of trousers that looked as though they would survive a nuclear war, hiking boots and a fluffy purple beret with a brooch in the shape of a Highland Cow pinned to one side.

Rose had rolled her eyes speechlessly when she opened the door to her.

"Do you like the brooch?" Bessie asked. "I thought the horns would make him feel at home."

"What on earth are you blethering about, you daft old woman?"

"Vikings – horns – helmets. You know."

"They didn't *have* horns on their helmets, Bessie."

"Oh. Didn't they? Never mind. He probably likes cows."

"I hope so," said Rose darkly, ushering her into the sitting room where Callie waited.

That had been nearly three hours ago, Callie realised, as the clock in the hall struck eleven. George, Julia and David had been sent to the cinema to keep them out of the way, but they'd be back soon. The room smelled unaccountably of vinegar. She wiped her sweaty forehead with her hand.

"Ready to try again?" Rose asked.

Not really. I'd like to sleep for about 24 hours now, would have been the truthful answer, but that wasn't an option. They were picking Josh up from the road end at East Neuk Cottages at one in the morning. Anna wasn't prepared to let him spend the night at The Smithy in case he was in the way. That meant Callie had less than two hours to get this right.

Rose and Bessie had somehow put two complex spells straight into her mind simply by joining hands with her, but it was one thing to know what the words were and another thing entirely to operate the spells correctly. Callie could tell the older witches were getting worried that it wasn't going to work, though they tried not to show it, so she summoned a smile and said, "Ready."

"You're still holding back too much," Bessie pointed out. "You need to surrender yourself to the spell, become part of it, not try to stay separate."

Callie nodded and began.

The candles burned with black flames. Callie drew them out and wove them into a seven-stranded rope, then wove the words of the prisoning spell into it as well, until the rope was so drenched in power that it sank to the floor under the weight of it.

She cut it loose from the candles with a gesture and brought the ends together with her mind, working the spell back and forth like a needle now to unite them until the rope formed a dense black circle.

That was the easy bit done.

She wiped her face again and moved the second spell to the front of her mind. The embedding spell. The one that could leave Josh stuck with some horrible remnant of Duncan Corphat for ever, if something went wrong.

"Callie?" Rose said quietly, bringing her back to where she should be.

I can do this.

Callie began to draw the rope tighter with her mind, imagining it containing and restraining all of Duncan Corphat's power. It shrank slowly, until it was the size of an armlet, heavy and dark as night.

She tried to gather all the power she had and pour it into the words of the embedding spell:

Let this power be held within my power
Let this power be mine to wield
Embed it in my helper
Let this power not hurt him
Let this power leave him when I so command
I will this. So let it be.

The black rope faded away and Callie stood in the centre of the room, drained.

"Better," said Rose. "Definitely better."

"Good enough?" Callie asked, not daring to hope.

"Have a break and we'll try once more," said Rose, dodging the question.

Josh was terrified he'd fall asleep and not wake up, and he didn't dare set the alarm on his phone in case his mum heard it, so when he said goodnight to Anna at half past eleven he sat on his bed, fully clothed, trying to make sure he didn't get too comfortable.

He read for a bit, but he couldn't concentrate. His heart rate was already higher than usual and his mouth was dry with nerves. Once again, he'd agreed to a crazy plan, and now he was regretting it. Why on earth had he said he'd do it? Even Callie thought he was nuts to say yes.

It was because of her, of course. Callie might be strange, but she was way more interesting than his friends back in Edinburgh. He'd just got caught up in the whole thing without having time to think. Until now. But he knew there was more to it than that. There was something special about Callie – nothing to do with her being a witch – that meant he didn't want to let her down. He cared about her; he didn't want her facing this alone.

The last crazy plan worked out okay, he told himself. *Sort of okay. Although it didn't go the way Rose and Bessie said it would.*

This'll be different.

This'll be worse.

+++

At a quarter to one, he put a torch and his Swiss Army knife in his pocket, opened his window wide and climbed out into the night. He didn't put the torch on, letting his eyes adjust to the dark instead. He could see the glimmer of a few lights in Pitmillie and the more distant general glow of St Andrews. There wasn't a sound from anywhere. Josh started towards the road a couple of hundred metres away, moving slowly at first, then with increasing confidence. He reached the road without incident and a few minutes later saw car headlights approaching.

"Evening," said Bessie cheerfully as he climbed into the back seat beside Callie. "Isn't this fun?"

"How are the spells?" he asked Callie.

"Fine," she said, not entirely truthfully. She knew that Rose and Bessie had their doubts about whether she could make them work, but there was no alternative and they'd run out of time.

"We'll drop you at the house then get down to Dane's Dyke and start work there," Rose said as she turned the car.

"How are *we* getting to Dane's Dyke?" Josh asked.

There was a horrified silence.

"We're getting too old for this," muttered Bessie.

"I'll have to get George, get him to pick you up," Rose decided.

"I thought you were trying to keep him out of this?" said Bessie.

"You don't have to involve George. I can drive Josh in our car," said Callie.

"Don't be ridiculous. You can't drive, and even if you could, it's not legal," Rose spluttered.

"I *can* drive, Rose. George taught me out at the old airfield eighteen months ago."

Rose slammed on the brakes and the car jolted to a halt in the middle of the road.

"George did *what*?"

"Please don't be angry with George. I nagged him for ages before he would do it."

Rose fumed silently.

"Can I just point out," said Bessie in a carefully neutral voice, "that compared with the other things we're hoping Callie will manage to do tonight, driving a car is pretty straightforward."

"But it's *illegal*," Rose pointed out.

"I'm fairly sure that messing about with graves and raising the dead is illegal too," Bessie pointed out.

"Whose side are you on?" Rose demanded.

"Callie's." Bessie looked her in the eye.

The car lurched forward again as Rose pressed the accelerator. Her silence was obviously all the consent Callie was going to get.

A few minutes later they were at Callie's house. Rose gave her a fierce hug. "Drive carefully," she said. "Are you sure you've got everything?"

Callie peered into the bag she was carrying and nodded.

Bessie put a hand on her shoulder. "Remember: let your power flow. Become *part* of the spell." She gave

Callie a peck on the cheek. "We'll see you later."

"Good luck," said Josh as the witches got back into the car.

"Luck's got nothing to do with it, young man," said Bessie, and then they were gone.

Callie and Josh stood alone in the darkness in front of the haunted house.

"Here goes nothing," said Callie, unlocked the door and reached forward to switch on the hall light.

They stood together on the doorstep, taking in what had been Callie's house.

Water dripped and trickled everywhere. The carpet had disappeared, replaced by a cratered, muddy floor. Stones poked incongruously through the wallpaper here and there, and the light fitting now hung from a roof of rock.

It seemed that Duncan Corphat was no longer content with the bedroom.

Rose parked the car as close to Dane's Dyke as possible, and she and Bessie set off on foot, using witch light as well as torches to show their way over the uneven ground.

"What do you suppose Barbara and Isobel would say if they could see us now?" mused Rose.

"They'd say we were a couple of old fools who'd forgotten our limitations," said Bessie after a few seconds thought. "But not to our faces, of course."

After five minutes they reached the line of the dyke, and scrambled onto the top.

"I wonder why John Fordyce took George to the grave all those years ago?" Bessie asked, catching her breath. "He should have known better than to show it to someone with no power. The whole point of all those spells that were put on it hundreds of years ago was to stop ordinary folk finding it."

"Well, he knew that George and I were courting and that I was a witch," Rose mused. "I'd always assumed he just thought it was all right because of that. But now, I wonder... John's family had the second sight as well. You don't think he could have had some sort of... foretelling... that George – or rather *we* – would need the Longman one day? I mean, did it never strike you as odd that George still remembers it all in such clear detail after all these years? Maybe John Fordyce *made* him remember."

"Well, it's certainly the sort of almost-useless way second sight usually works," said Bessie acerbically. "I mean, would it not have been easier to tell George not to let Callie go down the tunnel in the first place?"

They set off to find the grave.

Josh and Callie edged forward through the rocky passage that had been the hallway of her house. There was a fizz, and the lights flickered as water ran down the wire from the wet roof. Josh reached for his torch just as the lights died altogether. He fumbled with the switch and was relieved when it came on.

"I don't know how long that'll survive in here," Callie

whispered, and conjured a light of her own. She set it drifting along just ahead of them.

They had reached the stairs now, and found those, too, transformed to rock: narrow, steep and wickedly slippery. The light floated ahead of them as they climbed cautiously, Josh with his torch clamped between his teeth.

Upstairs, there was no sign that this had ever been a house: everything was rock or water or mud. There were no doorways, except for a narrow opening that led to what had been Callie's bedroom. Cold, dank air stirred their hair as they stood at the entrance.

They stepped inside.

The ball of witch light hung in the air in front of them, gradually penetrating to the corners of the rocky chamber – it was certainly no longer a room – they stood in.

Callie's broken bed stood incongruously in the middle of the uneven stone floor, the only trace of what had once been here.

Patches of darkness clung to the walls and roof here and there. Josh half thought he could hear a sound like breathing coming from them. His skin was clammy with fear. The rock chamber was watching them.

The torchlight faded to a thin ribbon of dim yellow light and died. Josh shoved the torch back in his pocket. Callie was a couple of steps ahead of him, standing quietly, taking in everything that gave her a clue to the power she faced. After a moment she knelt down and pulled from her bag the things she needed for the spells: the black-flamed candles, a tied bundle of birch twigs and a piece of paper with Duncan Corphat's name written on it in ink made from rowan berries.

As he watched Callie, Josh caught movement from the corner of his eye. He turned sharply and saw a blot of darkness creeping across the wall to his right to join with a smaller one.

"Callie," he whispered, "the darkness is moving."

16. DUEL

By witch light and starlight, Rose and Bessie looked down at the scrubby undergrowth at the seaward end of Dane's Dyke.

"Do we even know this is the right place?" asked Bessie, poking at leaves with the toe of a hiking boot.

"It's the place George saw the grave," replied Rose.

"So we're assuming it's got the decency not to roam around, anyway?"

"Yes we are." Rose closed her eyes, concentrating.

"Coo-ee! Anyone home?" Bessie called into the darkness, making Rose jump.

"Behave yourself, Bessie!" she said sharply. "Come over here and look for it properly."

Looking slightly chastened, Bessie went to stand by Rose's side, rummaged in her pockets and produced a pair of chopsticks.

Rose raised her eyebrows as she took one of them.

"I know – they're not traditional – but they work beautifully, and if we happen to magic up a bowl of noodles, we'll be equipped to deal with them," said Bessie brightly.

Rose opened her mouth to reply, but thought better of it. "Let's get on with it then," she said.

They separated, turned to face each other and held

out the chopsticks. Slowly they began to walk towards each other. At first the chopsticks did nothing, then they began to vibrate like tuning forks. The witches moved them around until they pointed in the direction that produced the strongest vibration, then sent witch light coursing through them.

The two beams of light crossed at a point near the highest part of the dyke. Rose and Bessie pointed the lights down at the ground where they intersected. Grass and nettles tore themselves out of the soil with a groan, revealing a long slab of featureless grey stone, under which, if legend was correct, the Longman lay waiting. Rose shivered, although the night was warm.

"That's going to take some shifting. It's a good job you thought to bring a crowbar," said Bessie, resolutely ignoring the fact that the hair was standing up on the back of her neck.

"I just hope we're strong enough to open it without using magic," said Rose, probing for the best spot to insert the end of the crowbar. "We don't want him expecting us." She settled the crowbar. "Right. Push here, Bessie."

They put all their weight on the end of the iron bar and were rewarded with a small sideways movement from the slab. After a few seconds they stopped pushing and Rose moved the bar to another spot. They shoved again and the slab moved a bit more.

"It's not enough," said Rose, peering at the gap they'd opened up. "It's going to have to be magic."

"Blast!" said Bessie. "I did so want to surprise him."

Rose put the crowbar down and they both pointed at the stone.

"Open," they told it.

With a noise of tearing roots the slab tilted up on one edge and fell backwards with a thud into the undergrowth.

They stared into the Longman's Grave.

Callie and Josh stood as far from the walls as they could, watching the patches of blackness creep and scuttle about and gradually draw together.

"It's Duncan," said Callie. "Keep watching it. I need to get the spell ready."

She swept a circle of the floor with the birch twigs and began to arrange the candles. Josh didn't know how she could let the darkness out of her sight. He watched it with uneasy fascination.

"Surely you should be paying attention to this, not the candles?" Josh hissed.

Callie gave him a puzzled look. "I need to get this right before I do anything else. Do what I told you!"

Josh stared at Callie, taken aback.

"Sorry," she said stiffly.

"Yeah. Me too."

Callie finished positioning the candles and got to her feet.

"I almost feel sorry for him," she said. "He was so desperate to escape, and all he's done is bring his prison with him."

You dare pity me, witch? said the rock around them, and the darkness coalesced into a great stain on the roof above them. *You would do better to fear me. This place is mine now.*

Callie lit the candles and began to weave the rope.

As cloud covered the stars, Rose and Bessie drew their witch lights closer to the grave. At first all they could see was a layer of sand sifted over whatever else it contained. As they watched, a wind sprang from nowhere and began to move the sand in little eddies, rising in thin, rotating columns like miniature whirlwinds, pouring and swooping out of the grave. They shielded their eyes from the stinging particles for a few seconds, and when they looked again, the sand was gone.

In front of them now lay a huddle of bones, broken and brown and spotted with age, jumbled together in a formless heap, broken shards showing white here and there. A stench of ancient death and decay rose from them, making Rose and Bessie take a step back, hands to their noses.

On top of the heap, brown and smooth and whole, sat a skull, with eye sockets full of night. The Longman looked out at the mortal world for the second time in living memory.

Josh's eyes flickered between Callie and the monstrous shape on the roof. The whole cavern seemed to breathe harshly around them now, as Duncan Corphat brooded over them. Josh watched Callie weave black flames into a loop of rope, without understanding anything of what she was doing. The rope settled to the floor and she set the piece of paper with Duncan's name in the centre of the circle it formed.

"Duncan Corphat," she said steadily, though her heart was hammering, "I conjure you. I know your true name and you must answer to it."

WITCH! screamed the room.

The blackness from the roof dropped into the circle, and Duncan Corphat unfurled himself from it, bloody and terrible.

Josh shrank back from the figure as it stood up, and up, towering the full height of the rocky chamber.

"Get out, witch," said the figure. "We will not tolerate your presence again. This place is ours now."

"You've dragged your prison with you, Duncan Corphat. You told me, down there in the dark under the castle. You told me you longed for air and light again. What good is this to you?"

"It is ours. It is all we have."

"You are all *dead*. You should be at peace, sleeping under the earth."

"There is no peace," the figure roared. "None for us. None for you."

"I can give you peace."

"LIAR!" The roar was so loud that it dislodged rocks from the walls.

"Callie – let's get out of here. You can't beat him, he's too strong," yelled Josh.

"Shut up, Josh. You don't know what you're talking about. Just shut up and keep out of this."

"*Keep out of this?* You need me or you can't do anything with him. Do you even know what you're doing? You're only a beginner. You can't do this."

"Shut up!" Callie screamed, and raised her hand sharply. Josh was flung back against the wall behind him and slid to the floor, winded.

"Just shut up," she said, more quietly.

Beyond her, Duncan Corphat laughed.

"Give up, witch-girl. You're no match for me and you know it."

Callie's resolve wavered. Rose and Bessie couldn't have properly understood what she would be facing, or they would never have thought she could do this. Why had she listened to them? They were nothing but foolish old women.

Sprawled on the floor, Josh tried to catch his breath. He saw Callie hesitate, saw the doubt in her eyes, and had a second of total clarity.

"Callie, it's him! He's putting the doubts into our minds. He's making us argue. We have to fight it. Don't listen to him."

What would he know? said Duncan Corphat inside her head. *He doesn't understand. How could he?*

She shook her head, trying to dislodge the insistent voice. There was something she had to do, but what was it?

Rose and Bessie stared wordlessly at the Longman's skull, chills running across their skin. The air above the grave hummed with power, making the grass around it shiver.

The witches looked at each other and nodded agreement, then released the spell from the grimoire that had written itself inside their flesh. The words rose like a cloud of tiny moths, settled on the heap of bones and sank gently into them.

There was profound silence for a few seconds, then a voice like bones grinding together came from the open grave.

"Why have you woken me?" it demanded. "Who dares wake the Longman and disturb the spirits he guards?"

"It worked," breathed Bessie. "Oh heavens."

In the grave, something moved, and the witches clutched at each others' arms apprehensively.

Something like a silver snake slid among the bones, growing larger and duller and fainter as it did so.

The Longman's bones began to shift. Shattered fragments reassembled themselves before Rose and Bessie's eyes as the bones drew themselves together, drew themselves up. Feet, legs, hipbones, a palisade of ribs; skeletal fingers flexed at the end of bony arms. With a click, the skull settled into place atop the spine and turned, with terrible slowness, towards the witches.

The Longman stepped from his grave.

"Callie. Callie, what's wrong?"

Josh's voice brought her back to herself with a jolt.

"Nothing. It's all right." She tried to concentrate on the rope, to begin to draw it tight around the spectre. With a terrible laugh, Duncan Corphat stepped out of the loop. He spread his arms, blood dripping from the wrecked stump of his left wrist.

"Was that meant to imprison me, witch-girl? It's a feeble thing. Is it your best?"

Behind the spectre, the stone walls began to burn. Josh could feel the heat on his face. He pulled himself to his feet, fought down his doubts.

"You can do it, Callie," he yelled. "Don't listen to him. I know you can do it."

Callie lifted the power-heavy rope with her mind, dropped it over the looming figure and began to speak the words of the embedding spell.

As the noose fell over him, Duncan Corphat cringed away from it, seeming to Josh to shrink. Hope surged in him as he heard Callie chanting the words of the spell. The fire had reached halfway across the room now. It licked at the rope and began to consume it. Duncan Corphat laughed again, bent, and tore the burning rope apart.

"You should have run when I gave you the chance," he roared, advancing on them.

"Who dares wake the Longman from the quiet of the earth?" demanded the voice of bones.

Rose gulped, but took a determined step towards the spectre.

"Rose Ferguson. I dare wake you by the power I command."

Bessie straightened her hat. "Bessie Dunlop. I dare wake you by the power I command."

The Longman stepped out of the air above the grave to confront them.

He was well named, for he stood almost two metres tall, even now: a brown skeleton clothed in the memory of flesh and armour and weapons. Fathomless eyes regarded them.

"Why have you broken my long sleep? No one has dared disturb me in many years. Why have *you* dared to do so? Why have you poured this power into my grave? Why have you broken my rest?"

"We need your help," said Rose.

Fire roared in front of Josh's eyes, Callie and the spectre outlined against it. He could see that she was trying to re-make the rope, her hands shaking as she did so. He had to do something to help her, but what? How could he buy her some time?

He shoved his hands in his pockets, feeling for... he didn't know what. His fingers closed around the useless torch and he pulled it out of his pocket. What good was a broken torch, though? Unless...

With clumsy fingers he unscrewed the end of the handle and tipped out the batteries. The spectre and the fire were only a couple of metres away from Callie and her half-made rope now.

"Callie, step back. I've got an idea," he said urgently. "Batteries and fire – think what will happen. It might distract him."

She nodded absently and took a step back, working the ends of the rope together. Josh lobbed the torch casing at Duncan Corphat's bloody face so he wouldn't notice as he flung the batteries into the fire behind him. For a few seconds nothing happened, then there was an explosion and a gout of yellow flame among the red. Caught unaware, Duncan Corphat's figure shrank, and in that instant Callie cast the new rope over him and without pausing, began to tighten it.

He's escaped twice. I will not let it happen again. Anger flowed through her like blood. *I will not let this happen.*

She gave herself up to the spell, let it take her and make her part of it. She ignored everything – Duncan, Josh, the burning room – and became the spell. She heard a scream, ignored it, let the spell and the power pour out of her.

Callie realised her eyes were closed and opened them. The room was full of smoke from the flames she had killed without even realising. A small, black circle lay on the floor, infinitely dense, heavy with power.

She lifted it with her mind. "Josh," she said, "come here."

When he stood by her side she slid the black loop over his right hand and saw him shudder as she sealed the spell and locked Duncan Corphat away inside him.

"It's done," she said flatly.

Side by side, illuminated only by witch light, they walked out of the shattered room.

+++

"We need you to take charge of another unquiet sleeper – one who has not accepted that he is dead," said Rose.

"Why?" demanded the old, cold voice.

"He is dangerous, full of power that he does not understand and cannot control. He's becoming more and more of a threat as his power grows. He must be contained before he becomes too powerful to stop."

"Deal with it yourself, witch-woman."

"I don't have the knowledge."

"You had the knowledge to wake me. That is surely enough?"

"No. I could fight him moment by moment, but we need a refuge for him, rest for the poor soul. He is not evil, just frightened and angry. Very angry. You have offered help to others in the past."

"That was long ago. My spirits lie quiet with me now. We sleep the long sleep of death at last. Why should I disturb their peace for you? You and your ghost are nothing to me. I am sworn to protect those who already lie beneath the earth with me. That is all." His tattered flesh, his rags of clothing blew away from him so that all that was left was his brown skeleton, bare, uncompromising.

"Leave me in peace. I will not help you."

The Longman began to drift back into his grave.

"No!" yelled Rose and Bessie, but he paid them no heed as he faded away, and left them alone in the night.

"We've failed," whispered Rose.

17. THE LAST BATTLE

Josh's head was full of mutterings. He tried to ignore them as they climbed back down the stone stair and moved towards the front door.

"Are you all right, Josh?" Callie asked anxiously.

He nodded, afraid to open his mouth in case someone else's voice emerged.

For a couple of metres around the front door, the house was still her house. The hooks where all the keys hung were still there, including – thank goodness – the car keys.

Callie snatched them down and shoved Josh out of the front door. She closed it firmly behind her, placed her hand on the door and spoke to it.

"You will not open again unless I tell you to."

Run, said a voice in Josh's head. *I can keep you safe from the witch.* With an effort, he ignored it, moving to the car like a sleepwalker.

"Get in," said Callie tensely.

Josh opened one of the back doors.

"Get in the front," she said as she opened the driver's door.

He had to speak then.

"I don't think I should, Callie. He's talking to me, trying to persuade me to do things. What if he made me grab the wheel?"

Callie gave him a long look, then nodded, and they both got into the car. Josh belted himself in, hoping that Duncan wouldn't know how to unfasten the catch. He saw Callie watching him in the rear-view mirror and tried to smile.

"It won't be long, Josh. He'll be gone soon."

He hoped she was right. If he let his mind wander for a second he could feel Duncan Corphat simmering just under the surface. He tried not to listen to the words as Callie turned the car, a bit jerkily, and set off tentatively towards the coast.

"Wait!" yelled Rose. "We summoned you. You can't leave like that."

"I am not yours to command, witch-woman," said the voice of bones from the grave.

"We're not trying to *command* you," said Bessie, thinking fast. "We ask this as a favour of you, Great Lord."

The grave gave a laugh like the scraping together of stones.

"Flattery will not move me either, witch-woman. Get you gone from here and leave me to my long sleep."

There was silence.

"Go faster," said Josh.

"No."

"Go faster."

Callie glanced in the mirror. Blue eyes stared angrily back at her. Not Josh's eyes, but Duncan's. She didn't dare turn round, concentrating on the road instead.

Surely the spell was strong enough to hold him? She looked at those eyes in the mirror again and found herself unsure.

Go faster, he said into her mind. *End it. Drive into a tree, into a wall. You would have peace. I would have peace. Let me go.*

"No!" yelled Callie. "I'm not listening."

She began to speed up.

Lean over, boy, said Duncan into Josh's mind. *Do it for her. Your witch friend is too weak. She does not dare. End this for all of us. She has joined us together to make a monster. She cannot undo this. She lacks the power. This is the only way we can be free. Take the wheel. End it.*

Josh unfastened his seatbelt.

"What do we do now?" Bessie asked, looking at the bones in the grave.

"What we told Callie. We'll just have to let him loose out here. Take your last look at Dane's Dyke, Bessie," Rose said in a defeated voice. "We'll not be visiting again for a long time."

She looked, in vain, for any sign of car headlights.

"They're taking too long. Something's happened."

"What are you doing? Josh, answer me!" Callie yelled.

"What you cannot," said Duncan Corphat's voice.

Callie looked round wildly and saw Josh reaching for the handle of the door. She slammed her hand down on the central-locking button.

"Fight him, Josh. Put the seatbelt back on." She didn't dare turn round again on this bit of road. In the rear-view mirror, Josh's brown eyes looked back at her, and she felt a surge of relief. "That's it, Josh. You're winning," she said encouragingly. "Put the seatbelt back on." She slowed down for a tight curve. "We're nearly there."

She had to concentrate now so she wouldn't miss the narrow turn-off. There it was. A few more minutes and she'd be able to hand all this over to Rose and Bessie.

The car bumped along the rough ground of the track that led to Dane's Dyke.

"It's just ahead, Josh. Josh?"

With a snarl, Josh threw himself forward and grabbed the wheel.

"There they are," said Rose with relief. She and Bessie watched the beam of the headlights move jerkily towards them along the track for a few seconds, then suddenly swing wildly off to the right.

"Oh no," Rose whispered. "Please, no."

The car had come to rest with one of the back wheels in the ditch, bonnet pointing up at the dark sky.

As Rose and Bessie puffed their way towards it, the driver's door opened a bit.

"Callie!" yelled Rose.

"I'm okay," came the muffled response. The door opened a little more, and Callie pulled herself out.

Rose threw her arms round her granddaughter.

"Duncan – Josh – grabbed the wheel," Callie said.

Bessie peered into the back of the car. Josh was sprawled on the floor, eyes open, looking dazed.

"Is he hurt?" asked Bessie.

Callie pulled herself away from Rose and hauled open the back door.

"Josh?" she said. He looked at her and rubbed his jaw. "I hit him," said Callie to no one in particular. "Well, punched him, really. Duncan made him grab the wheel. I had to stop him."

"That was quite a punch," said Josh groggily, and started to pull himself out of the car. The others took a step backwards.

"It's me," he said reassuringly. "For now, anyway. He's gone quiet."

"You did it, you clever girl," said Bessie. "Well done. We knew you had it in you."

"Admit it, though – you had your doubts."

"Yes, we did," admitted Rose.

"We shouldn't be standing around here talking," said Callie, anxious to finish things as quickly as possible. "Did you raise him?"

"Yes," said Rose. "But he refused to help."

"Why?" asked Callie, aghast. She'd assumed that Rose and Bessie could do anything if they put their minds to it.

"He wasn't exactly communicative," said Bessie.

"Well, let's try again now. Surely if we show him Duncan he'll realise how important it is that he takes him?"

"He was pretty clear."

"No. We have to try again."

"You're right, Callie. You've done what you had to," said Rose. "We can't give up now. Come on."

Callie turned off the headlights and they made their way back towards the dyke.

"Josh – is it still you? Keep talking to me."

"It's me, but I know he's still in here. I can feel him watching, if that doesn't sound too crazy."

"Tell me if anything changes."

"Okay."

They tramped along the dyke to the grave. It still lay open, abandoned in haste when Rose and Bessie had seen the car go off the road, the Longman's skull grinning atop its pile of bones.

"Call him out again," said Callie.

Rose and Bessie looked at each other and released the waking spell again. The spell sank into the Longman's bones and the cold voice spoke once more as the silvery snake shape slipped out from his skull.

"You dare wake me again? You were warned to leave me in peace, witch-women."

Rose opened her mouth to speak, but to her surprise Callie moved in front of her as the Longman stepped from his grave again, rags and tatters blowing in a wind that wasn't there.

"I made them call you back. You must take this spirit into your keeping."

"*Must?* You try to command me, witch-child? Perhaps I shall take you down into the grave instead."

"No you won't," said Callie steadily, as the others watched, astonished. "I *do* command you, by the power I bear. But more than that: if you refuse to do this then I say you are a coward. You are afraid of the spirit that I have imprisoned. Your power is no match for it, and no match for mine." She hardly recognised herself as she spoke, had no idea where this bravery had suddenly come from.

Wind howled out of the grave, tearing at Callie's clothes and hair.

"I fear no spirit!" thundered the apparition. "I fear no *witch*." He spat out the final word, raised a ghostly sword, and strode towards her. "You are mine, witch-child," he growled.

"No," she said calmly. "You are *mine*."

She raised her hands and let power flood into her.

"I command you by the power in my flesh, by the power in my blood, by the power in my bones," she shouted, and the air around her ignited. "I command you by the power of the earth and of the air and of the sea."

Rose gasped and started forward, but Bessie grabbed her arm to stop her.

"You can't help her, Rose. She's too deep in the magic."

Rose said nothing, staring in anguish at her granddaughter.

A vortex of silver fire howled around Callie. She fought to keep her footing as the power funnelled into her and through her, streaming from her hands with a noise like a peal of thunder. It struck the Longman square in the chest, forcing him back towards his grave.

"Do as I say. Take Duncan Corphat down to the underworld and keep him there. Do as I say or I'll blast your bones and your grave to dust and you will never know rest again."

"Callie, he's..." Josh's voice was suddenly cut off, as Duncan Corphat, sensing the danger he was in, made one last bid to escape.

"Stop what you're trying to do, girl." Josh stepped in front of her. "I will be free, even if I have to kill your friend."

In Josh's hand was his Swiss Army knife, the open blade at his own throat. Duncan's malevolent blue gaze was fixed on Callie's face. Behind her, she heard Rose and Bessie gasp.

"Never mind your spells, you filthy witches. I can cut his throat before you can say them."

The flow of power from Callie's fingers slowly died away and for a moment there was perfect stillness. The Longman's spectre hung suspended in midair. For a few seconds, Callie was frozen with fear for Josh then, somehow, she knew what she must do.

"Are you sure you want to be trapped in a corpse?" she asked Duncan coldly. "Kill him and I can't break the spell that binds you to him."

"Liar!" shrieked Duncan, but Callie saw doubt make his blue eyes waver for an instant to Josh's brown ones.

"Put the knife down and I'll undo the spell," she said.

"Swear it!"

"I swear I will undo this spell as soon as you put the knife down."

Duncan took the knife from Josh's throat and lowered his arm, but he didn't fold the blade away.

"Do it," he rasped.

Callie stepped towards Josh and spoke the words to release the black armlet from his wrist. She slid it off and it blew away like smoke.

"There," she said. "You're free, just as you wanted."

As Callie watched, Josh sank to his knees. Behind him stood Duncan Corphat in all his baleful, bloody power, blue flame crackling round him, a smile of ferocious joy on his ruined face. She turned to the Longman.

"Take him," she commanded.

Duncan Corphat sprang snarling into the black air, but the Longman was on him before he had time to do anything. He swung his great shadow-sword straight through Duncan's insubstantial body. For a second, nothing happened, then Duncan Corphat broke apart into a million tiny flakes of darkness that were sucked, shrieking, into the Longman's sword.

The Longman regarded Callie from his empty eye sockets. "I have done your bidding. I have obeyed the Wild Magic. Do not presume to disturb my rest again," he said.

He stepped into his grave, flesh and clothes and sword gone now, and his bones tumbled and settled and sank into the earth. The stone slab lifted and tilted and crashed down to close the grave, and the Longman and Duncan Corphat were both gone.

It was a couple of minutes before anyone moved or spoke, then Callie turned round to face the others.

Rose and Bessie stared at her in frank amazement from where they stood. Josh was still on his knees. As Callie watched, he threw down the knife with a shudder. She walked to where he knelt, and dropped to the ground beside him. They threw their arms round each other.

"I'm so sorry," she said. "I'm so sorry. I didn't really understand about the power before. I never knew what he could do. I never knew what *I* could do. I understand now."

He hugged her tighter for a few seconds, then pushed her away and held her at arm's length.

I knew it, she thought. *I've lost him. He hates me for letting that happen to him.* Then she realised he was smiling.

"That," he said slowly, "was incredible. *You* were incredible. He's gone. You made that... that... the Longman do what you wanted. Amazing." He was staring at her as though he'd never seen her properly before.

With difficulty, she pulled her gaze away to Rose and Bessie. They were staring at her too. Suddenly she began to feel embarrassed, and was thankful that no one could tell in the pale witch light that her face was scarlet.

She slowly disengaged herself from Josh's hands and got to her feet.

"What?" she said. "Stop staring at me as though I've got two heads. I just did what you taught me."

"Nobody taught you to do that, child. Nobody could have," said Bessie in wonder.

"No one has *ever* forced the Longman to do something against his will," added Rose. "No one except you." She shook her head as if she was dazed.

"See what happens when you surrender to the spell and let the power flow? That's what we've been *trying* to teach you for months," Bessie said, recovering herself.

Josh picked up his knife and closed it carefully, put it back in his pocket and got to his feet.

"We should go," said Rose.

"What about our car?" said Callie, remembering suddenly.

"We'll get it pulled out of the ditch in the morning," said Rose as they walked.

"Once we've concocted a good story to explain how it got there," cautioned Bessie.

Inside the car, Callie pushed back her sleeve. The mark on her wrist had vanished. She held up her arm so the others could see. "Look. I felt it go, somehow, when the Longman took Duncan."

No one spoke much as Rose drove mechanically back to Pitmillie. It was half past three when they dropped Josh as close to East Neuk Cottages as they dared.

"See you later," said Callie softly as he got out.

The cottage was silent as he climbed back into his room, undressed and crawled into bed.

I'll never get to sleep, was his last waking thought.

18. AND THEN...

Callie had gone, yawning, to bed as soon as they got back to The Smithy, but Rose and Bessie sat over cooling cups of tea in the kitchen, talking quietly as Bessie waited for daylight before she drove back to St Andrews.

"All that power..." Bessie shook her head. "I'm glad we didn't realise how much she had when we started to teach her. I'd have been afraid to let her in my house in case she accidentally reduced the whole thing to rubble. I never thought for a moment she'd be able to channel Wild Magic out there. Earth and air and sea... good grief."

"Nor did I," said Rose. "I've never seen *anyone* use Wild Magic like that." She paused, then said, "I don't think we should let her know just yet how... exceptional she is."

"Heavens, no. She's only just got to grips with the idea that she's got any power at all. We'll have to take it slowly, but, my goodness, what she'll be able to do..."

"What will she *choose* to do, I wonder?" Rose took a swallow of tea and grimaced. "Cold," she said, and got to her feet to pour it away.

"All that can wait for now. I just need to tidy things up here: take the spell off Julia and David, try to make my peace with Julia, do what I can to help sort out the house..."

"Mere details," said Bessie airily.

It was early afternoon. Julia and David sat reading in the garden of The Smithy, still happily enspelled, George pottering beside them. Their car had been retrieved, more or less undamaged and sat in the road outside The Smithy, waiting for Rose to take it back. She and Callie had decided to have a look at the state of Callie's house before they decided what to do next.

When they got there, Callie opened the door and hung back to let Rose enter first. Rose stood in the hall, looking round in disbelief. Callie had warned her what to expect, but...

But the house was simply a house, not the claustrophobic set of chambers and tunnels into which Duncan Corphat had transformed it. Rose and Callie walked silently from room to room. The sitting room was still littered with butchered photographs and the contents of the cupboards sat on the kitchen floor. David and Julia's room was a maelstrom of clothes and the tarpaulin flapped over the hole in Callie's ceiling, but otherwise there was no trace of what had happened.

"How can it look like this now?" asked Callie, baffled.

"It must all have been illusion," Rose replied.

"But it was real."

"No, Callie. It *felt* real. You saw for yourself last night just what power can do." She turned to face her granddaughter. "Concentrate for a minute: how does the house *feel* now?"

Callie closed her eyes. "Normal. Empty. He's definitely gone."

Rose smiled. "I think we should have a bit of a tidy up before your parents get here."

They spent an hour setting the place to rights as much as they could, then Rose called George to bring Julia and David home.

"I'll take the spell off them and then..." Rose gave a sigh, "and then we'll try to explain."

Callie's heart sank at the prospect. "Rose," she said hesitantly, "if it gets too bad with Mum – about me being a witch – can I come and stay with you and George?"

"You know you can."

"I don't mean just for a few days."

"I know you don't, dear. Let's hope it doesn't come to that." They heard the sound of a car engine. "Here they come. I'll put the kettle on."

"Hello, dear," said Julia as she came in. "It *is* nice to be home."

"Hello, Callie," said David. "Cup of tea? Lovely."

George, coming in behind them, raised his eyebrows at Rose.

"Everything's fine," she said.

"I think I'll go and see if anything in the garden needs watering," he said, heading for the back door. "David might want to come out in a few minutes."

"I'm sure he will," said Rose.

The four of them sat round the kitchen table. "Here

goes," said Rose, putting her hands flat on it. She looked from Julia to David. "I release you," she said simply.

Callie watched as her parents realised properly where they were, looking round in confusion as though they had just woken up. She saw in their faces vague memories of what had happened : what they had said, what they had done.

They looked at each other, and at Callie, in anguish.

"It's all right. None of it was meant. None of it was your fault," said Rose reassuringly. "Everyone's safe. There's nothing that can't be put right."

"What happened to me?" pleaded David. "Have I been ill? Have I been mad? Why did I think those things?"

Rose leaned forwards and clasped his hands. "David, listen to me. I know you don't understand what's happened to you, but believe me when I say it's over. It will never happen again. Your family is safe." She released his hands and sat back. "Now, please go into the garden and have a talk with George. He'll explain all the things that it's better he and you don't know anything about."

David looked at her as though she was mad.

"Go on. George will make sense of it for you."

There must have been some trace of the compulsion left, for David meekly did as he'd been told.

Julia put her face in her hands. "I can't bear it," she sobbed. "How could I have thought those things? How could I have said them?"

"It wasn't you, dear. Callie and I know that. There was something else in the house, making you do those things, twisting your thoughts, twisting your feelings."

Julia took her hands away from her face. "I dreamed of someone," she said. "In the house with us. So angry. So frightened." She shook her head. "But I can't... Oh, Callie!"

Callie threw her arms round her mother. "It's all right," she said. "I understand."

"Drink your tea, Julia," said Rose, "and we'll try to explain it all. It might take a while."

Rose and George had gone, leaving Callie alone with her parents. They kept glancing at her when they thought she wouldn't notice.

"Stop it!" she said suddenly. "I feel like something in a zoo."

David turned her to face him and gave her a hug.

"I had an interesting talk with George," he said, choosing his words carefully, "about things that he and I don't know anything about. It explained quite a lot about your gran and your mum that I'd never quite understood. And it explains a lot about you." He set Callie back at arm's length. "You marvellous girl." He grinned. "And that, apparently, is all I have to say about things."

Callie smiled back at him, more relieved than she could express. At least one parent had accepted her for what she was.

"I'm starving," David went on. "Who's for fish and chips?"

"Yes."

"Yes, please."

"I'll nip down to Anstruther and get them then." He kissed his wife and daughter before he left.

It was as good a time as any for the difficult conversation, Callie decided.

"Mum," she began, "I understand if it's too hard for you, having me around here."

Julia stopped what she was doing and stared at her daughter. "What do you mean?"

"All the witch stuff. I could move out, go and stay at The Smithy."

"Is that what you think I want?"

"I... I don't know."

Julia sat down. "All those things I said..."

"I know you didn't mean them. Rose explained. It was Duncan."

Julia shook her head. "Not just that. I mean the way I've been since you discovered you're a witch." She gave a shaky laugh. "I'd been dreading it for years."

Callie's heart sank.

Julia saw her expression. "No – I don't mean it like that." She took a breath. "I never understood why I wasn't like Mother. So when you were born and she told me you might be, I was worried. If you were both witches, where did that leave me? I was afraid you wouldn't need me. I was jealous."

She groaned. "I can't believe how pathetic that sounds. Jealous of my own mother and daughter. I know mothers are supposed to be embarrassing, but that's way past any reasonable limit. I wouldn't be surprised if you *did* want to go and stay at The Smithy after that."

"I don't, though. As long as you can cope with having me here," Callie said carefully.

"Of course I can cope. Just don't go putting one of those spells on me again, like Mother did."

"As long as you behave."

"Careful." Julia wagged a finger. "Just because you're a witch doesn't mean you can be cheeky."

She sobered.

"You've been so brave, Callie. You saved us all. No one else could have done it. Not even your grandmother."

"Beginner's luck," said Callie, embarrassed by the unfamiliar praise. "It was the most amazing feeling, down at Dane's Dyke. It was like being part of... of everything in the world. I was fighting against being a witch until last night, but I'm not ashamed of what I am any more. It's part of me. A marvellous part of me."

"I know," said Julia, smiling.

Josh and Callie lay on their backs on the baking sand, watching the single tiny white cloud in the sky.

"Go on. Make it move." Josh elbowed her in the ribs.

"Don't be daft. I can't."

"How do you know? Go on, try."

Callie squinted up at the cloud for a few seconds. It stayed still.

"There. Satisfied? I'm not a performing monkey, you know."

"Okay. You'll have to work on that a bit before I see you again. Remember, I'll be expecting to be impressed."

He sat up. "I suppose I'd better go and help Mum pack up. We're meant to be leaving in an hour."

"And so another peaceful country holiday draws to its close," Callie intoned solemnly as she sat up too.

"Yeah. Even more boring than the last one. Your dead relations don't half cause a lot of bother up here. I think it would be safer if you came to Edinburgh for a holiday next time."

"Is that an invitation?" Callie screwed up her face. "Edinburgh? Nothing to do there. I'd get bored." She shrieked with laughter as he started to tickle her.

As they walked up the road from the beach, Josh asked, "Do you think you'll manage to use your superpowers only for good once you're back at school with all the idiots?"

"Mnnn... It's going to be hard to resist the temptation to give things a bit of a tweak sometimes, but Rose is very insistent that I mustn't do anything like that."

"But she won't be there watching you."

"This is true," said Callie with a mischievous smile. "You know, I'm quite looking forward to seeing Evie again."

Josh groaned. "Poor Evie."

They had reached Callie's house now, and sat down next to each other on the wall.

"Want to come in?"

"I'd better not. I was meant to be back half an hour ago. She'll be going mental as it is."

"Remember to put your photos up on Facebook."

"Yeah. I'll do it tonight."

There was an awkward silence for a few seconds.

"It's a shame we're too old for 'What I did on my holidays' at school now," Josh said to break it.

"We'd only get in trouble for making stuff up."

Conversation dried up again.

"Look, I'd really better go."

"I know."

"You're going to come down to Edinburgh for the September weekend, aren't you?"

"If I haven't been invited to some fabulous party here."

"I'll definitely see you, in that case. Are you coming on your broomstick?"

"Of course, and the cat'll be riding behind me."

"Don't wear the pointy hat, though. You'd look stupid in Edinburgh."

"I could turn you into something, you know."

"No you couldn't. You haven't got that far in *Witchcraft for Dummies* yet."

"I'll be working on it for September."

"Right. I'll remember not to be so rude then."

"Sure you won't be too busy trying to be cool to talk to me in Edinburgh?" She remembered what he'd said before any of this happened.

"Nah. You're pretty cool, you know. Why else would I have taken all those crazy risks and let myself be taken over by an angry ghost. You're..." He went a bit red, gave a lopsided smile.

There was a short silence, then Callie gave him an affectionate shove. "I thought you had to go?"

"I do." Josh got to his feet. "Bye then."

"Bye."

"See you in September. And remember, no pointy hat."

Callie smiled as she watched him walk away.

AUTHOR'S NOTE

All the settings I used in *Dark Spell* really exist in and around St Andrews, although I did take some liberties with the geography of Fife Ness.

You can walk along Dane's Dyke (though you'll probably be as unimpressed with it as Josh was), but you won't find Longman's Grave, even though it appears on maps. George's tale of being shown the stone slab and skeleton and never finding it again is a true story that happened to a friend of mine. I couldn't get it out of my head once I'd heard it (and I haven't been able to find the grave either). Fife is a strange and wonderful place!

The tunnels under St Andrews Castle are very creepy and well worth a look if you're visiting. Take a torch, just in case...

+++